# Author's Note

This novel has hand-drawn art from the author <3 I hope you enjoy them!

Also, The Royal's Saga Book-Box Set is now available for sale! You can order them from the author directly on Instagram, Tiktok, Facebook, or by email, listed in the "About the Author" section.

Each book-box includes all 13 Author-Signed novels, both Author-Signed novellas, specialized author prints, specialized bookmarks for each book, and lots of other little goodies and gifts included in each box, wrapped in beautiful packaging! Selling for $375 (Includes shipping, handling, and delivery to you.)

The Hard-Covers, which include more art and specialized covers, and extra gifts in the box.

Selling for $425 (Includes shipping, handling, and delivery to you!)

Get your book-box set ordered today!

# The Royal's Behind the Scenes

## Written by Kristen Elizabeth

## Table of Contents:

| | |
|---|---|
| Author's Note:........................................................... | 1 |
| Table of Contents:..................................................... | 2 |
| The Apathetic Knight Muse Playlist–......................... | 22 |
| The Apathetic Knight Muse Playlist–......................... | 25 |
| The Apathetic Knight Muse Playlist–......................... | 28 |
| Family Tree - Kyeareth ............................................. | 31 |
| Family Tree - Kyeareth ............................................. | 32 |
| Family Tree - Kyeareth ............................................. | 33 |
| Family Tree - Cinder ................................................. | 40 |
| Family Tree - Winter ................................................. | 41 |
| Map ........................................................................... | 42 |
| Character Profiles..................................................... | 45 |
| Character Profiles..................................................... | 48 |
| Character Profiles..................................................... | 51 |
| Character Profiles..................................................... | 54 |
| Character Profiles..................................................... | 57 |
| Story Timeline .......................................................... | 60 |
| The Villainous Princess Muse Playlist ...................... | 66 |
| The Villainous Princess Muse Playlist ...................... | 69 |
| Family Tree - Karmindy............................................. | 72 |

Family Tree - Karmindy ................................................. 73
Character Profiles ......................................................... 74
Character Profiles ......................................................... 77
Character Profiles ......................................................... 80
Story Timeline .............................................................. 83
The Disregarded Dragon Muse Playlist .................. 89
Family Tree .................................................................. 91
Family Tree .................................................................. 92
Character Profiles ......................................................... 93
Character Profiles ......................................................... 96
Story Timeline .............................................................. 99
The Hidden Queen   Muse Playlist ...................... 104
Family Tree ................................................................ 106
Family Tree ................................................................ 107
Character Profiles ....................................................... 108
Character Profiles ....................................................... 111
Story Timeline ............................................................ 114
The Conquering Empress   Muse Playlist ............. 119
Family Tree ................................................................ 121
Family Tree ................................................................ 122
Character Profiles ....................................................... 123
Character Profiles ....................................................... 126
Character Profiles ....................................................... 129
Character Profiles ....................................................... 132
Character Profiles ....................................................... 135
Story Timeline ............................................................ 138
The Abandoned Prince   Muse Playlist ................. 143

| | |
|---|---|
| Family Tree | 145 |
| Map | 146 |
| Character Profiles | 149 |
| Character Profiles | 152 |
| Story Timeline | 155 |
| The Decoy Duchess  Muse Playlist | 160 |
| Family Tree | 162 |
| Character Profiles | 163 |
| Character Profiles | 166 |
| Character Profiles | 168 |
| Character Profiles | 171 |
| Story Timeline | 174 |
| The Empathetic Brother Muse Playlist | 179 |
| Family Tree | 181 |
| Character Profiles | 182 |
| Character Profiles | 185 |
| Character Profiles | 188 |
| Story Timeline | 191 |
| The Anonymous Writer Muse Playlist | 195 |
| Family Tree | 197 |
| Character Profiles | 198 |
| Character Profiles | 201 |
| Story Timeline | 204 |
| Requested Bonus Chapter: | 206 |
| Ashid Zaron… | 208 |
| The Luxurious Slave Muse Playlist | 226 |
| Family Tree | 228 |

Family Tree ................................................................. 229
Character Profiles ...................................................... 230
Character Profiles ...................................................... 233
Character Profiles ...................................................... 236
Character Profiles ...................................................... 239
Story Timeline ............................................................ 242
Story Connections & "Easter Eggs"… ..................... 248
Dove ............................................................................. 260
Books by Kristen Elizabeth ....................................... 268
Acknowledgments ..................................................... 270
About the Author ....................................................... 272
What to look forward to in the next saga: ........... 279
Final Remarks ............................................................. 281

# The APATHETIC Knight

**PART I**

## The Crowning

# The Apathetic Knight Muse Playlist–

(Alphabetical Order)

## Book 0.5 theme: Three Day's Grace – Never Too Late

1. ASTAROTH theme: Somaticism – Symphonic Planet
2. Breaking Benjamin – Breath
3. Breaking Benjamin – Rain
4. CINDER theme: Flames in the Sky – Virtuocity
5. Citizen Soldier – Through Hell
6. Disturbed – Divide
7. Disturbed – Leave it alone
8. Duncan Laurence – Arcade
9. Ellie Goulding – Beating Heart
10. Evanescence – Bring me to life
11. Evanescence – End of the Dream
12. Evanescence – Like you
13. Gabbie Hanna – Dandelion
14. Hawthorne Heights – Dandelions
15. If Not For Me – Blameless
16. KYEARETH theme: Finding You – Symphonic Planet
17. Linkin Park – Pieces
18. Linkin Park – Pushing me away
19. Linkin Park – Runaway
20. Linkin Park – Sometimes I remember
21. Madonna – Frozen

22. Ruth B., (sped up and slowed) – Dandelions
23. SERYN theme: Warrior Theme – Avenged Sevenfold
24. WINTER theme: Bangalore – Symphonic Planet
25. WITCHZ – The Magic
26. Within Temptation – Blue Eyes
27. Within Temptation – Forgiven

# The Apathetic Knight

## Part 2
### The Burning

# The Apathetic Knight Muse Playlist–

*(Alphabetical Order)*

## Book 1.0 theme: Jeris Johnson & BOI WHAT – Battling My Demons

1. ASTAROTH theme: Somaticism – Symphonic Planet
2. Breaking Benjamin – Breath
3. Breaking Benjamin – Rain
4. CINDER theme: Flames in the Sky – Virtuocity
5. Citizen Soldier – Through Hell
6. Disturbed – Divide
7. Disturbed – Leave it alone
8. Duncan Laurence – Arcade
9. Ellie Goulding – Beating Heart
10. Evanescence – Bring me to life
11. Evanescence – End of the Dream
12. Evanescence – Like you
13. Gabbie Hanna – Dandelion
14. Hawthorne Heights – Dandelions
15. If Not For Me – Blameless
16. KYEARETH theme: Finding You – Symphonic Planet
17. Linkin Park – Pieces
18. Linkin Park – Pushing me away
19. Linkin Park – Runaway
20. Linkin Park – Sometimes I remember
21. Madonna – Frozen

22. Ruth B., (sped up and slowed) – Dandelions
23. SERYN theme: Warrior Theme – Avenged Sevenfold
24. WINTER theme: Bangalore – Symphonic Planet
25. WITCHZ – The Magic
26. Within Temptation – Blue Eyes
27. Within Temptation – Forgiven

# The Apathetic Knight

## PART 3

### The Freezing

# The Apathetic Knight Muse Playlist–
## (Alphabetical Order)

### Book 1.5 theme: Rain City Drive – Frozen

1. ASTAROTH theme: Somaticism – Symphonic Planet
2. Breaking Benjamin – Breath
3. Breaking Benjamin – Rain
4. CINDER theme: Flames in the Sky – Virtuocity
5. Citizen Soldier – Through Hell
6. Disturbed – Divide
7. Disturbed – Leave it alone
8. Duncan Laurence – Arcade
9. Ellie Goulding – Beating Heart
10. Evanescence – Bring me to life
11. Evanescence – End of the Dream
12. Evanescence – Like you
13. Five Finger Death Punch – Wrong Side of Heaven
14. Gabbie Hanna – Dandelion
15. Hawthorne Heights – Dandelions
16. If Not For Me – Blameless
17. JT Music – Nightmares Never End
18. KYEARETH theme: Finding You – Symphonic Planet
19. Linkin Park – Pieces
20. Linkin Park – Pushing me away
21. Linkin Park – Runaway

22. Linkin Park – Sometimes I remember
23. Madonna – Frozen
24. Ruth B., (sped up and slowed) – Dandelions
25. SERYN theme: Warrior Theme – Avenged Sevenfold
26. WINTER theme: Bangalore – Symphonic Planet
27. WITCHZ – The Magic
28. Within Temptation – Blue Eyes
29. Within Temptation – Forgiven

# Family Tree - Kyeareth

## Ashland/Severing:

**(DIRECT Paternal LINE ONLY)**

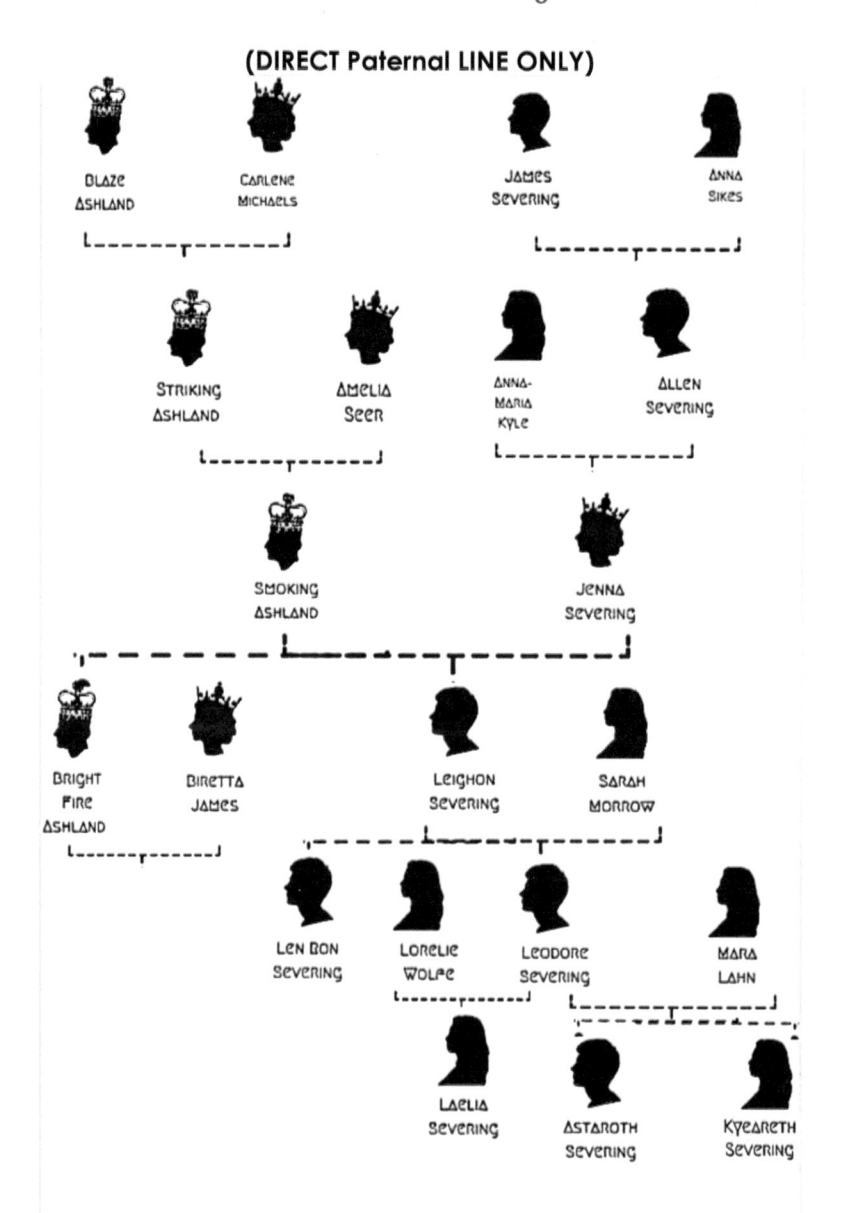

- Blaze Ashland — Carlene Michaels
- James Severing — Anna Sikes
  - Striking Ashland — Amelia Seer
  - Anna-Maria Kyle — Allen Severing
    - Smoking Ashland — Jenna Severing
      - Bright Fire Ashland — Biretta James
      - Leighon Severing — Sarah Morrow
        - Len Bon Severing
        - Lorelie Wolfe — Leodore Severing — Mara Lahn
          - Laelia Severing
          - Astaroth Severing
          - Kyeareth Severing

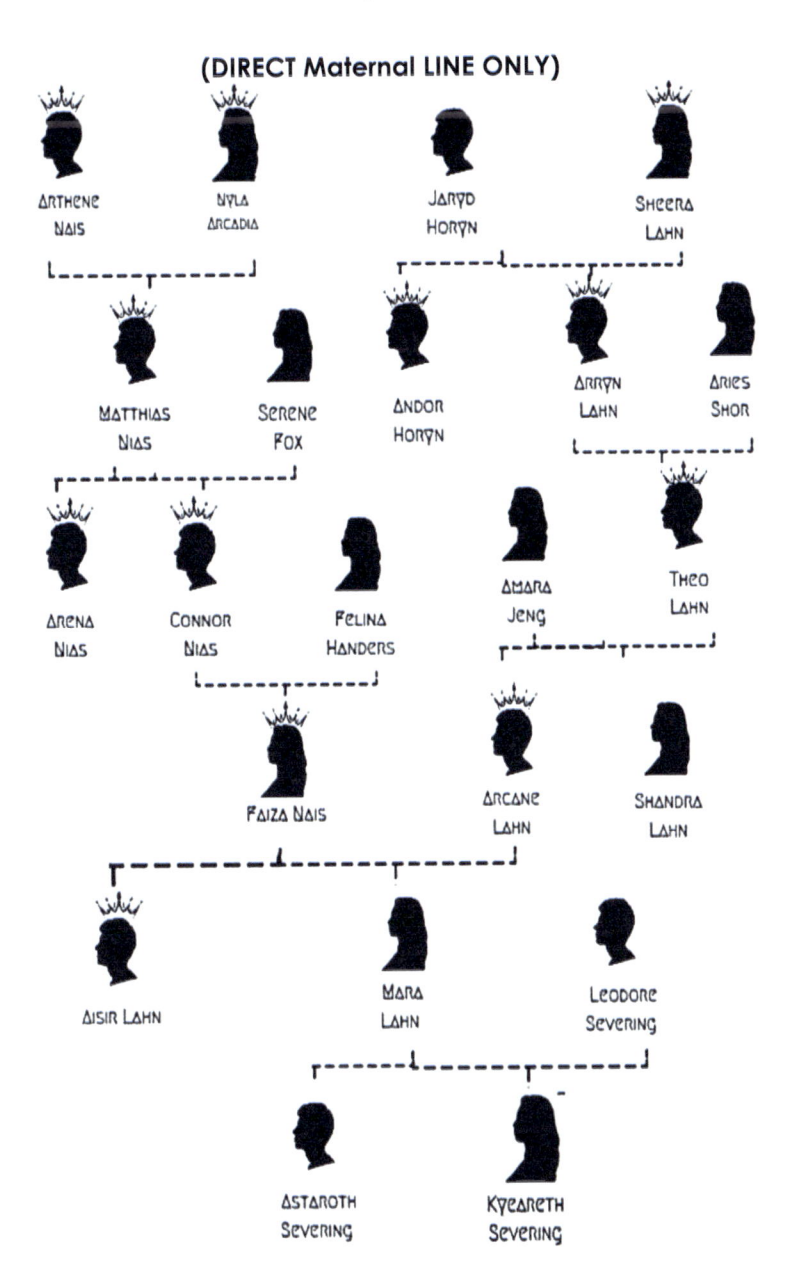

# Family Tree - Kyeareth

## Nias/Lahn:

**(DIRECT Maternal LINE ONLY)**

- Arthene Nais
- Nyla Arcadia
- Jaryd Horyn
- Sheera Lahn

- Matthias Nias
- Serene Fox
- Andor Horyn
- Arryn Lahn
- Aries Shor

- Arena Nias
- Connor Nias
- Felina Handers
- Amara Jeng
- Theo Lahn

- Faiza Nais
- Arcane Lahn
- Shandra Lahn

- Aisir Lahn
- Mara Lahn
- Leodore Severing

- Astaroth Severing
- Kyeareth Severing

17

# Family Tree - Kyeareth

## Children:

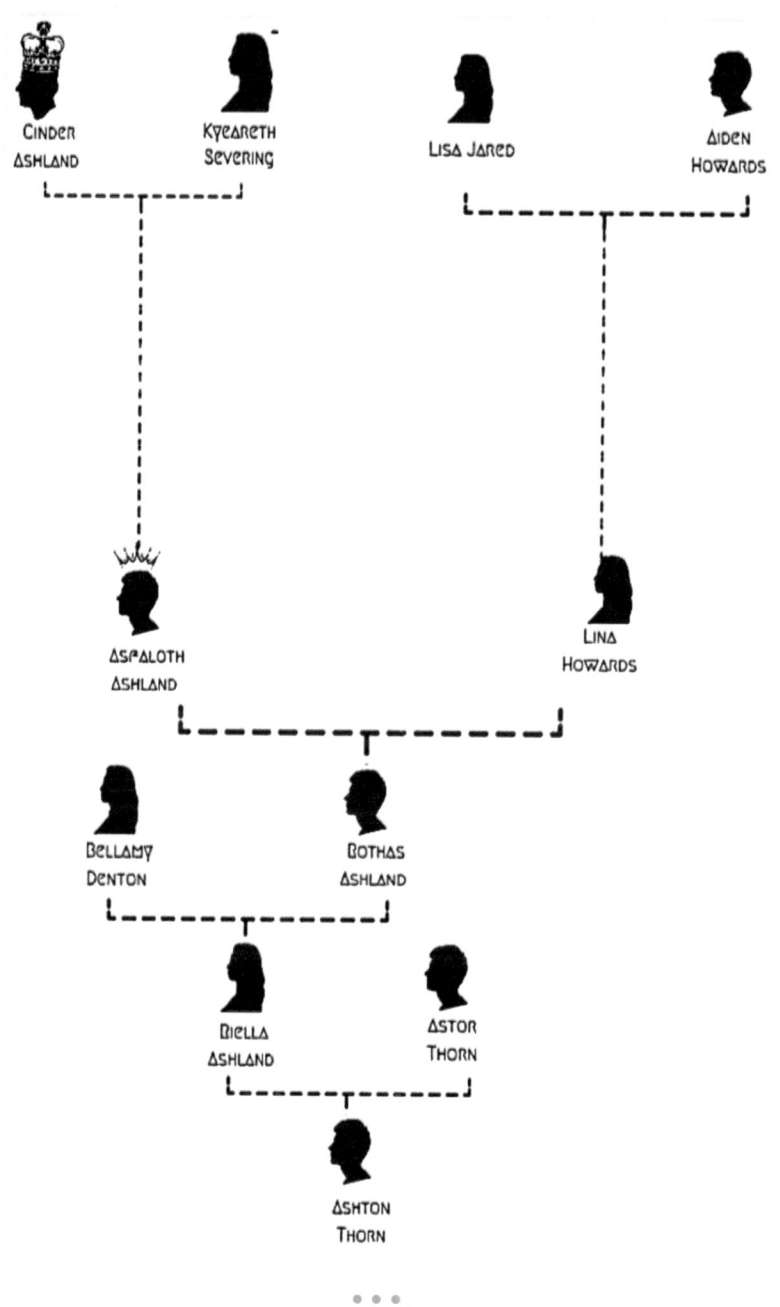

- Cinder Ashland
- Kyeareth Severing
- Lisa Jared
- Aiden Howards
- Aspaloth Ashland
- Lina Howards
- Bellamy Denton
- Bothas Ashland
- Biella Ashland
- Astor Thorn
- Ashton Thorn

18

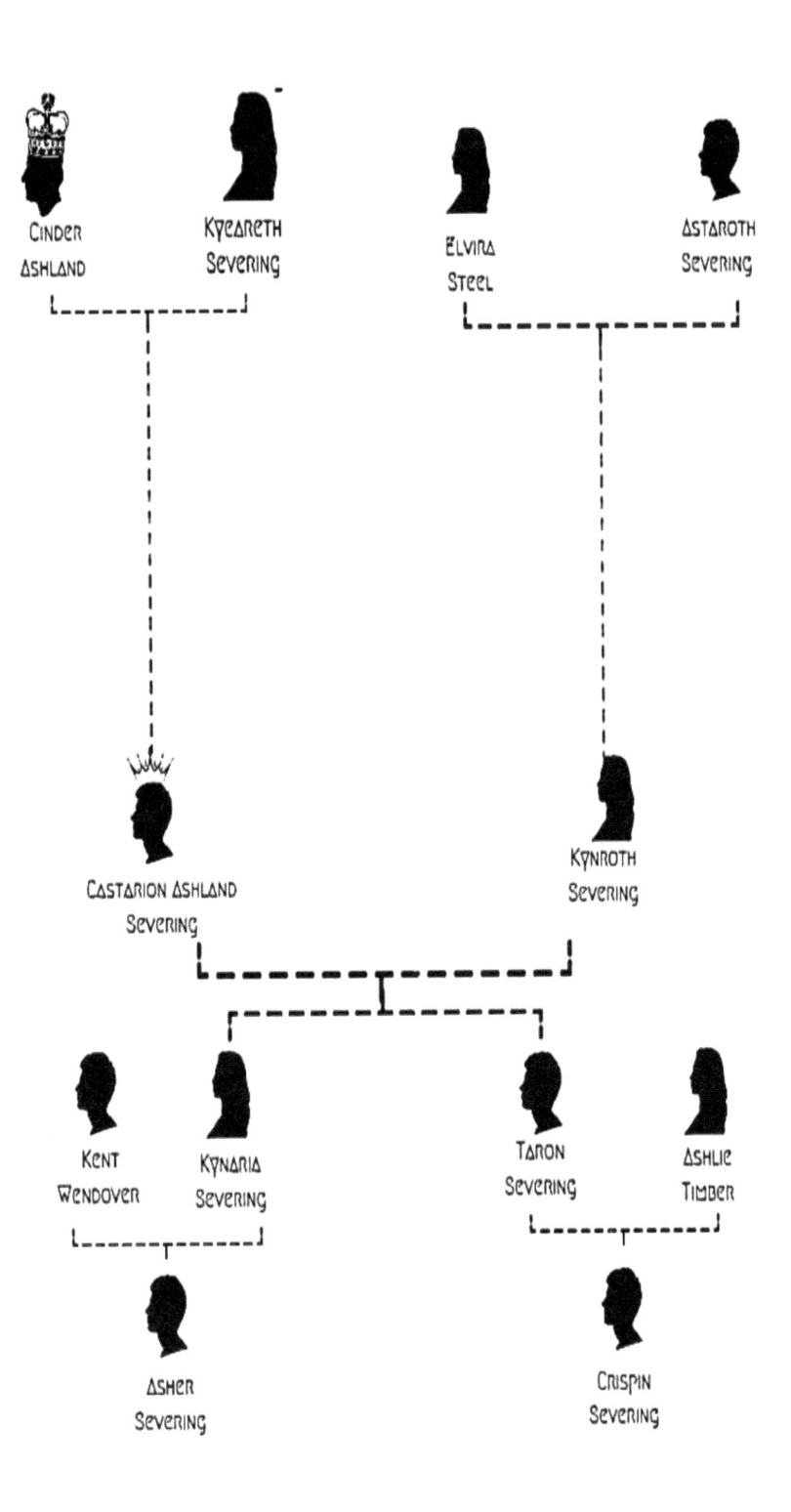

```
                Cinder         Kyeareth                    Elvira         Astaroth
                Ashland        Severing                    Steel          Severing
                   └──────────────┘                           └──────────────┘
                          │                                          │
                          │                                          │
                          │                                          │
                  Castarion Ashland                              Kynroth
                      Severing                                   Severing
                          └──────────────────────┬───────────────────┘
                                                 │
                   ┌──────────────┬──────────────┴──────────────┬──────────────┐
                 Kent          Kynaria                        Taron          Ashlie
               Wendover        Severing                      Severing        Timber
                   └──────────────┘                              └──────────────┘
                          │                                          │
                        Asher                                     Crispin
                       Severing                                   Severing
```

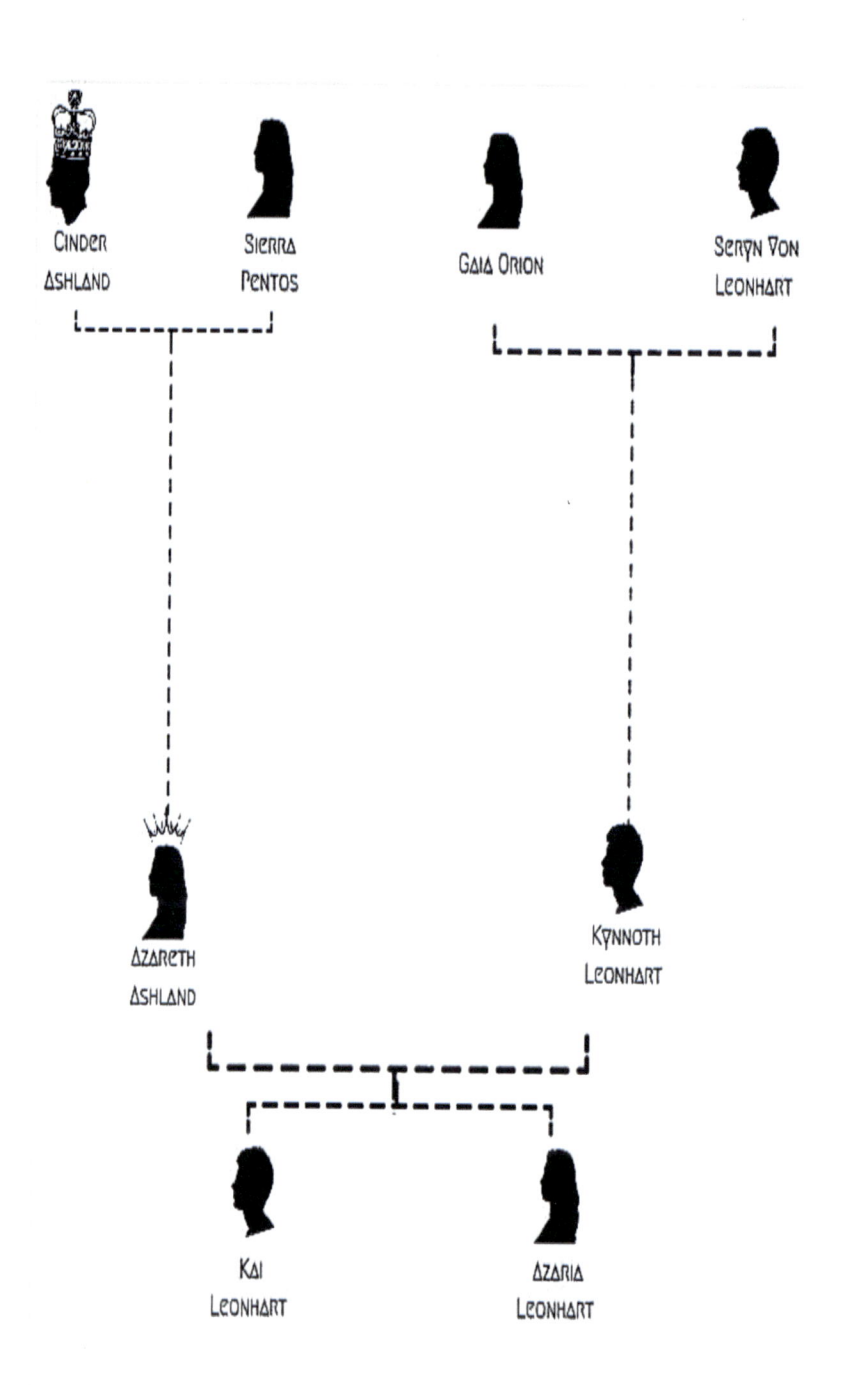

# Family Tree

- **Cinder Ashland** — **Sierra Pentos**
  - **Azareth Ashland**
- **Gaia Orion** — **Seryn Von Leonhart**
  - **Kynnoth Leonhart**

**Azareth Ashland** & **Kynnoth Leonhart**
- **Kai Leonhart**
- **Azaria Leonhart**

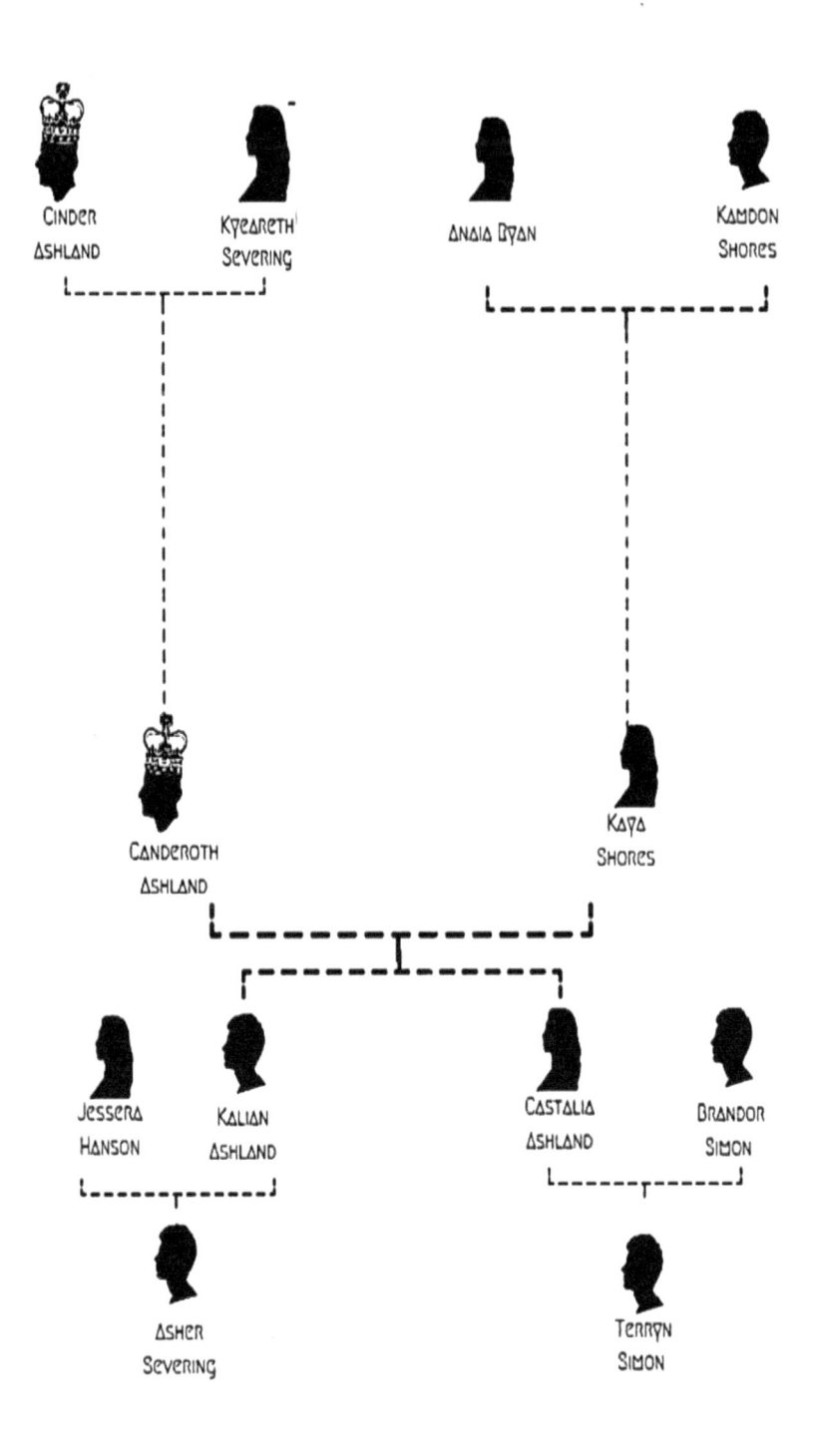

```
                Cinder          Kyeareth                Anaia Ryan              Kamdon
                Ashland         Severing                                        Shores
                   └───────────────┘                         └───────────────────┘
                           │                                          │
                           │                                          │
                    Canderoth                                        Kaya
                    Ashland                                         Shores
                        └──────────────────┬──────────────────────────┘
                   ┌──────────────┐                    ┌──────────────┐
                Jessera      Kalian                  Castalia      Brandor
                Hanson       Ashland                 Ashland       Simon
                   └──────┬───────┘                     └──────┬───────┘
                        Asher                               Terryn
                        Severing                            Simon
```

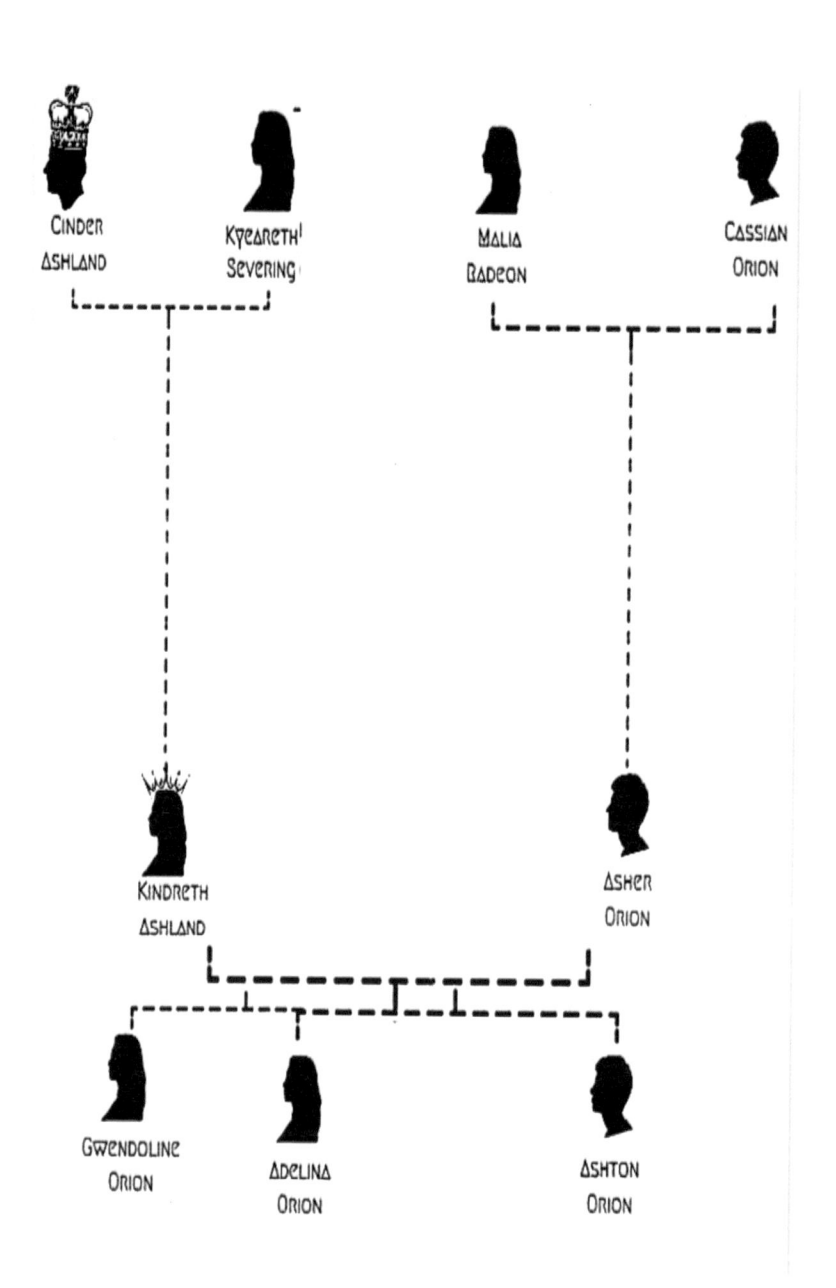

Cinder
Ashland

Kyeareth
Severing

Malia
Badeon

Cassian
Orion

Kindreth
Ashland

Asher
Orion

Gwendoline
Orion

Adelina
Orion

Ashton
Orion

Kyeareth
Severing

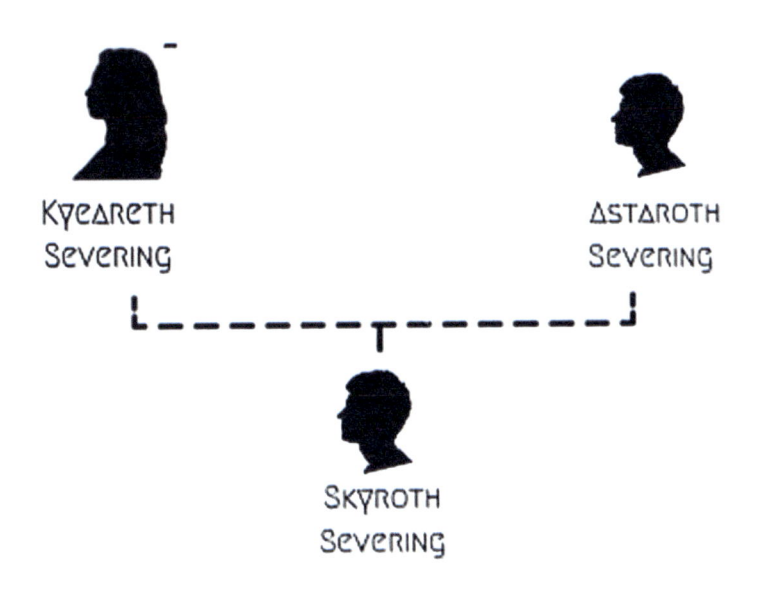

Astaroth
Severing

Skyroth
Severing

## Severing Family Tree

- **Kyeareth Severing** — **Winter Nias "Severing"**
  - **Snow Severing** — **Kayliana Briggs**
    - **Margaret Shandon** — **Storm Severing**
      - **Selene Severing** — **Baelyn Valoran**
        - **Johanna Caius** — **Jolan Valoran**
          - **Kenneth Valoran** — **Mila Thracian**
            - **John Valoran**
    - **Noel Severing** — **Olivier Anderson**
      - **Arisa Cavallaracion** — **Blizzard Severing**
        - **Arya Severing** — **Klein Duran**
          - **Maeve Leonhart** — **Andren Severing**
            - **Maevyn Severing**
            - **Maelstrom Leonhart**

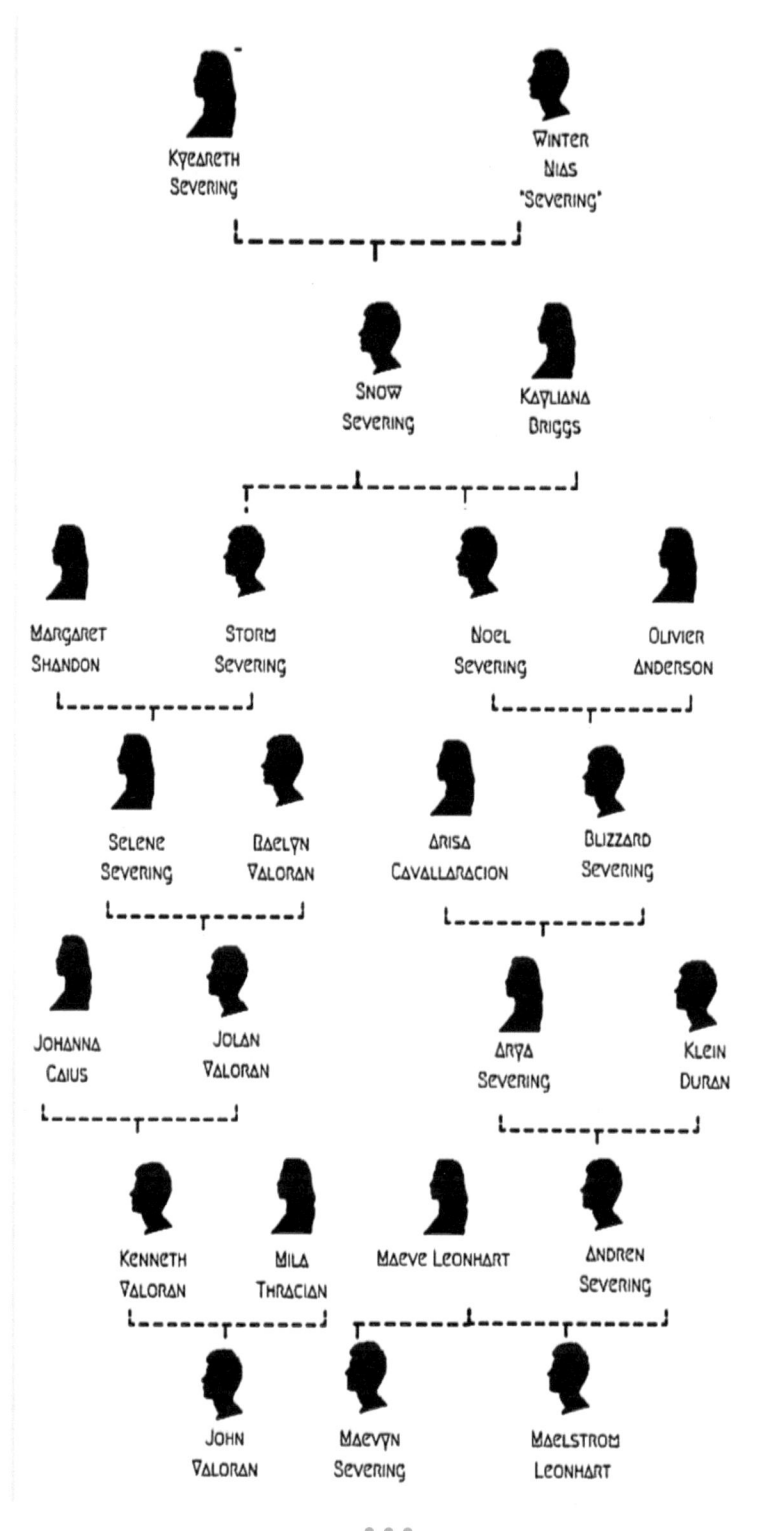

24

# Family Tree - Cinder Ashland

## (DIRECT Paternal LINE ONLY)

- Blaze Ashland
- Carlene Michaels
- James Severing
- Anna Sikes

- Striking Ashland
- Amelia Seer
- Anna-Maria Kyle
- Allen Severing

- Smoking Ashland
- Jenna Severing

- Bright Fire Ashland
- Biretta James
- Leighon Severing
- Sarah Morrow

- Cinder Ashland
- Flaming Ashland
- Ember Ashland
- Len Bon Severing
- Lorelie Wolfe
- Leodore Severing
- Mara Lahn

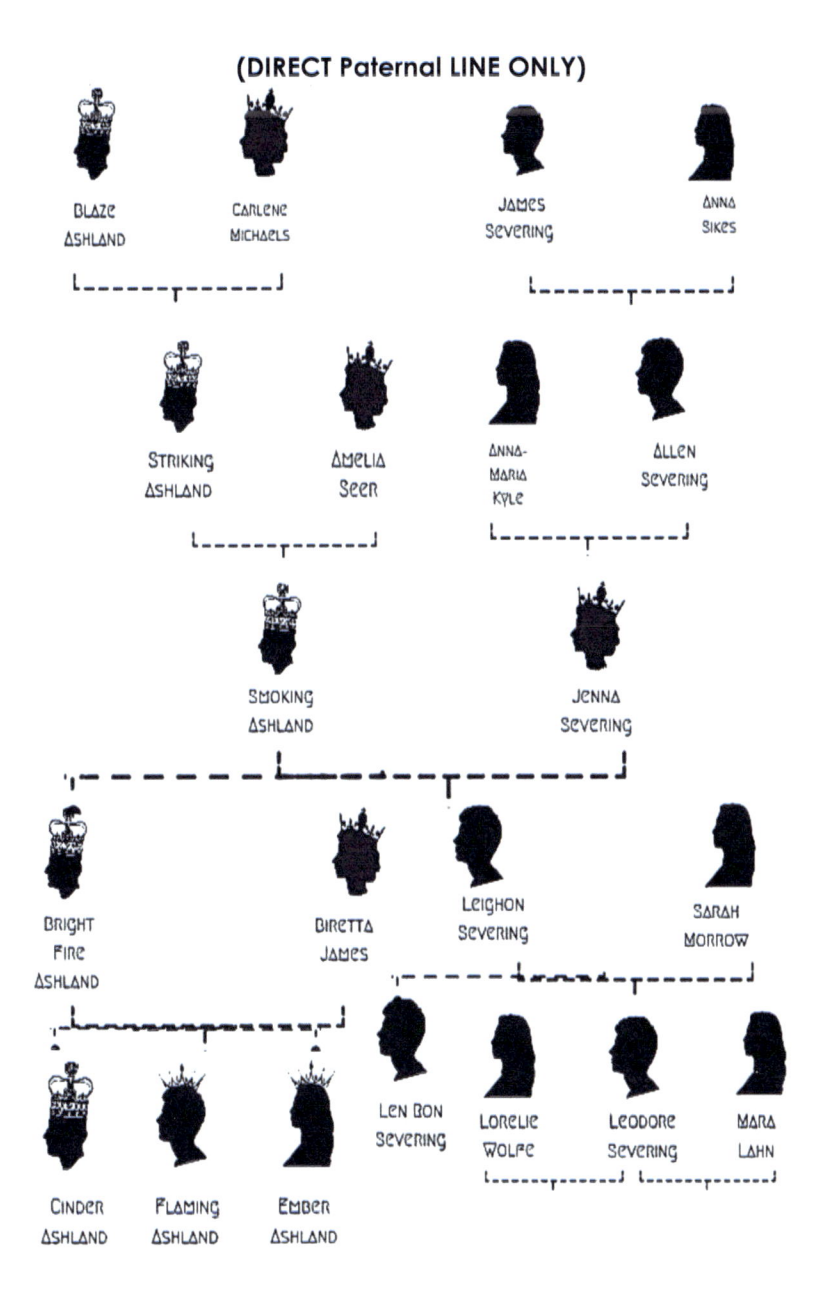

25

# Family Tree - Winter
## Arcadia / Nias

**(DIRECT Paternal LINE ONLY)**

- Aaryn Arcadia — Marie Kipling
- Varia Nias — Damien Vintner
- Lucian Vas — Vienna Arcadia
- Vinter Nias
- Drake Nias — Amber Canon
- Veyra Arcadia — Vinhos Arcadia — Lumina Haze
- Vanden Knight — Irina Nias
- Arene Jacobs — Levar Arcadia
- Shara Kentos — Marlia Nais — Darin Stagg
- Elrien Arcadia — Jasmine Marring
- Amina Hering — Marlyn Nais
- Nyla Arcadia — — — — — — — — Arthene Nias
- Serene Fox — Matthew Nias
- Stormy Taring — Arena Nias — Connor Nias — Felina Handers
- Winter Nias "Severing"
- Faiza Nais

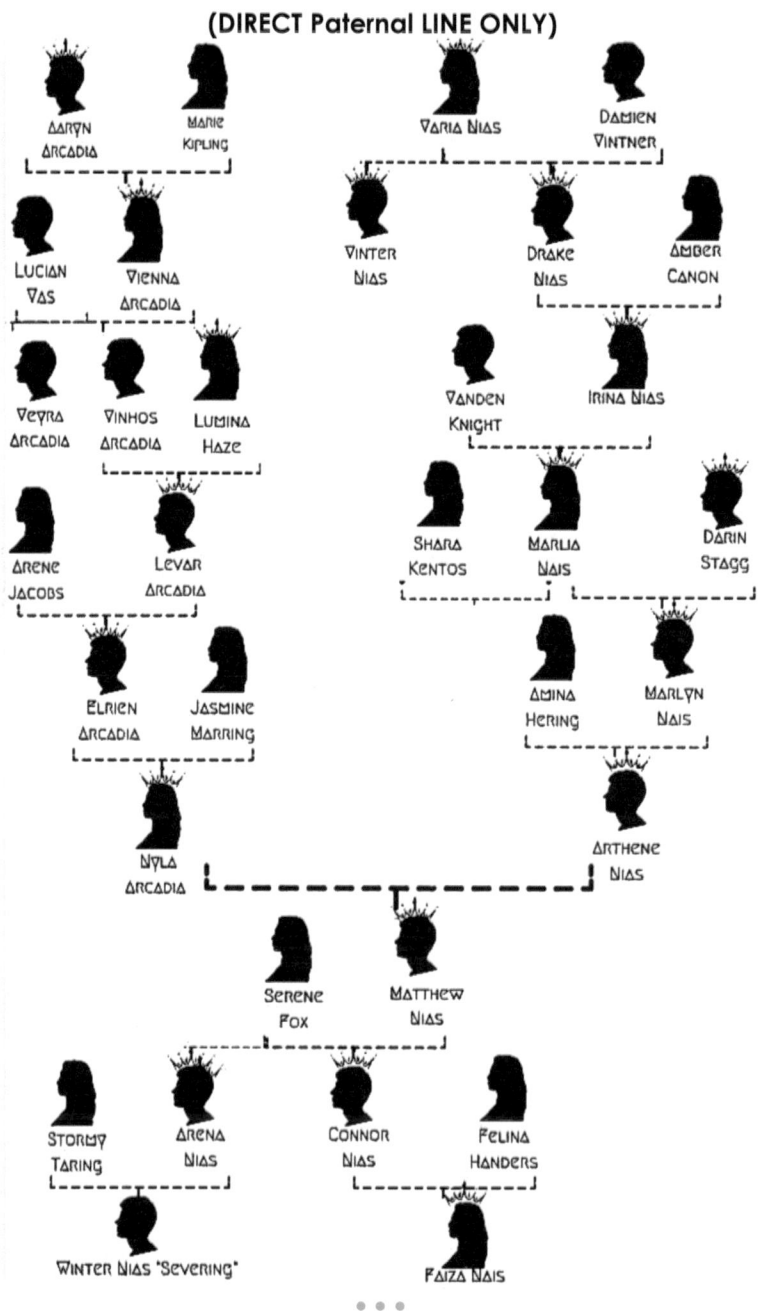

26

# Map

## Ashland Kingdom

28

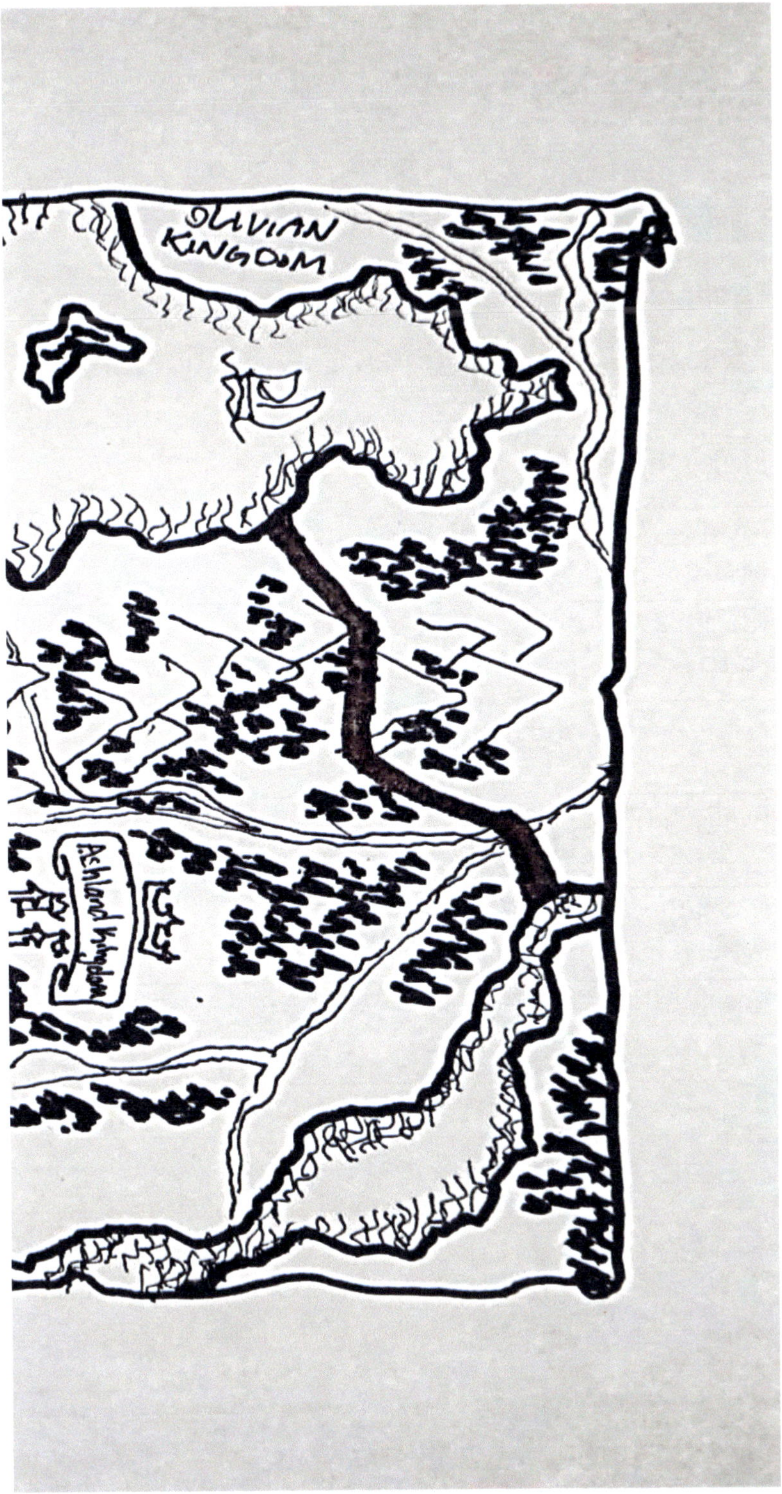
OLIVIAN KINGDOM
Ashland Kingdom

# Character Profiles

## Kyeareth

**Birthdate:** Solaris's Reign, 300 Ashland Rule

**Faction:** Mage-Born

**Rankings:** Duke's daughter, Crown Princess, Queen, Dowager Queen

**Stats Chart:**

| | | | | | | | | | |
|---|---|---|---|---|---|---|---|---|---|
| Mage Mana | █ | █ | █ | █ | █ | █ | █ | | |
| Knight's Aura | █ | | | | | | | | |
| Adaptability | █ | █ | █ | | | | | | |
| Battle Skill | █ | █ | | | | | | | |
| Magic Ability | █ | █ | █ | █ | █ | | | | |
| Intellect | █ | █ | █ | █ | █ | █ | | | |

# Character Art

# Realistic Art Character Inspiration

# Character Profiles

## Astaroth

**Birthdate:** Solaris's Reign, 300 Ashland Rule

**Faction:** Knight Faction

**Rankings:** Duke's son, Duke, Archduke

**Stats Chart**

| | | | | | | | | | | |
|---|---|---|---|---|---|---|---|---|---|---|
| Mage Mana | | | | | | | | | | |
| Knight's Aura | | | | | | | | | | |
| Adaptability | | | | | | | | | | |
| Battle Skill | | | | | | | | | | |
| Magic Ability | | | | | | | | | | |
| Intellect | | | | | | | | | | |

Character Art

## Realistic Art Character Inspiration

# Character Profiles

## Cinder

**Birthdate:** Folias's Blessing, 295 Ashland Rule

**Faction:** Knight's Faction

**Rankings:** Crown Prince, King

**Stats Chart**

| | | | | | | | | | |
|---|---|---|---|---|---|---|---|---|---|
| Mage Mana | | | | | | | | | |
| Knight's Aura | | | | | | | | | |
| Adaptability | | | | | | | | | |
| Battle Skill | | | | | | | | | |
| Magic Ability | | | | | | | | | |
| Intellect | | | | | | | | | |

## Character Art

# Realistic Art Character Inspiration

# Character Profiles

### Winter

**Birthdate:**

**Faction**

**Rankings**

**Stats Chart**

| | | | | | | | | |
|---|---|---|---|---|---|---|---|---|
| Mage Mana | | | | | | | | |
| Knight's Aura | | | | | | | | |
| Adaptability | | | | | | | | |
| Battle Skill | | | | | | | | |
| Magic Ability | | | | | | | | |
| Intellect | | | | | | | | |

# Character Art

## Realistic Art Character Inspiration

# Character Profiles

## Seryn

**Birthdate:** Year's Fall, 294 Ashland Rule

**Faction:** Knight's Faction

**Rankings:** Duke's son, Keeper Knight, King of Western Kingdom

**Stats Chart**

| | | | | | | | | | |
|---|---|---|---|---|---|---|---|---|---|
| Mage Mana | | | | | | | | | |
| Knight's Aura | ■ | ■ | ■ | ■ | ■ | ■ | ■ | ■ | ■ |
| Adaptability | ■ | ■ | ■ | ■ | ■ | ■ | ■ | ■ | |
| Battle Skill | ■ | ■ | ■ | ■ | ■ | ■ | ■ | ■ | ■ |
| Magic Ability | | | | | | | | | |
| Intellect | ■ | ■ | ■ | ■ | ■ | ■ | ■ | ■ | |

## Character Art

# Realistic Art Character Inspiration

# Story Timeline

## 3752 United Coalition Rule

**Veras's End:** Veyra and Sheane copulate

**Solaris's End:** Sheane's brother tries to kill Veyra's family, Sheane kills herself after discovering her pregnancy, Veyra and his mother are executed – Veyra's brother escapes.

## 3769 United Coalition Rule – Comes to an End. Ashland family takes over, bringing us to 001 Ashlan Rule.

## 149 Ashland Rule

**Solaris's End –** Branding receives Nyla as a "gift of sacrifice, he refuses this and gives her to her husband to be.

## 286 Ashland Rule

**Veras's End –** Leodore Severing is ordered by the king to overthrow Duke Severing on the battlefield and take over the duchy.

## 295 Ashland Rule

**Folias's Blessing –** Cinder Ashland is born

## 300 Ashland Rule

**Solaris's Reign –** Astaroth and Kyeareth Severing are born

## 313 Ashland Rule

**Solaris's Reign** – Kyeareth takes Seryn as her keeper Knight

## 314 Ashland Rule

**Solaris's Reign** – Astaroth marries Elvira, Kyeareth marries Cinder and is named Crowned Princess

## 315 Ashland Rule

**Solaris's Gifts** – Asfaloth Ashland is stillborn

## 317 Ashland Rule

**Nivis's End** – Kyeareth discovers pregnancy, Cinder is called away to war, Kyeareth chooses her Shadow Guardians, Coup happens, Kyeareth is "killed."

### MOVING TO BOOK 1.5 – TAK PART 2

**Seed's Sewn** – Kyeareth lands in Olivian Kingdom with no memory, rescued by Cassian and Gaia Orion, Kynroth Severing is born

**Veras's Height** – Cinder arrives for Kyeareth

**Solaris's End** – Castarion Ashland is born

## 318 Ashland Rule

**Solaris's Reign** – Astaroth named Archduke, Castarion named Astaroth's heir to the duchy and renamed "Castarion Ashland Severing."

## 319 Ashland Rule

**Solaris's Reign** – Kyeareth miscarries, memory returns

## 320 Ashland Rule

**Blizzard's Reign** – "new wife" consort brought in

**Seed's Sewn** – Kyeareth discovers pregnancy, runs away from Cinder to Astaroth, Astaroth arrested, Kyeareth runs from Severing Archduchy, leaves for Olivian Kingdom

**Veras's Height** – Lands in Olivian Kingdom

**Moon's Dance** – Azareth Ashland is born, Canderoth and Kindreth Ashland are born, Asfaloth is resurrected through Dark Magic

**Year's Fall** – Skyroth Severing is born

## 321 Ashland Rule

**Seed's Sewn** – Winter and Kyeareth become an official couple

**Solaris's End** – Winter proposes to Kyeareth and they marry

## 330 Ashland Rule

**Solaris's End** – Castarion and Kynroth come of age and become officially engaged

**Moon's Dance** – Canderoth is named Crowned Prince

## 338 Ashland Rule

**Solaris's End** – Castarion turns 21, becomes Archduke Severing, officially married to Kynroth Severing

## 341 Ashland Rule

**Moon's Dance –** Canderoth turns 21 and is named King

## 350 Ashland Rule

**Moon's Dance –** Canderoth is voted to become the first named Emperor of the new Central United Empire, creating a new Calander year.

## 001 Central Imperial Year

**Blizzard's Reign –** Empire's 5 kingdoms decided, as listed:

Central Kingdom – ruled by Canderoth/ imperial family

Northern Kingdom – Given to Duke Cassian, named King of the North

Southern Kingdom – Given to Kyeareth and Winter, named King and Queen of the South

Eastern Kingdom – Given to Eclipse Ren, named King of the East

Western Kingdom – Given to Seryn Leonhart, named King of the West

## 247 Central Imperial Year

**MOVING TO THE ROYAL'S SAGA BOOK 2:**

**THE VILLAINOUS PRINCESS**

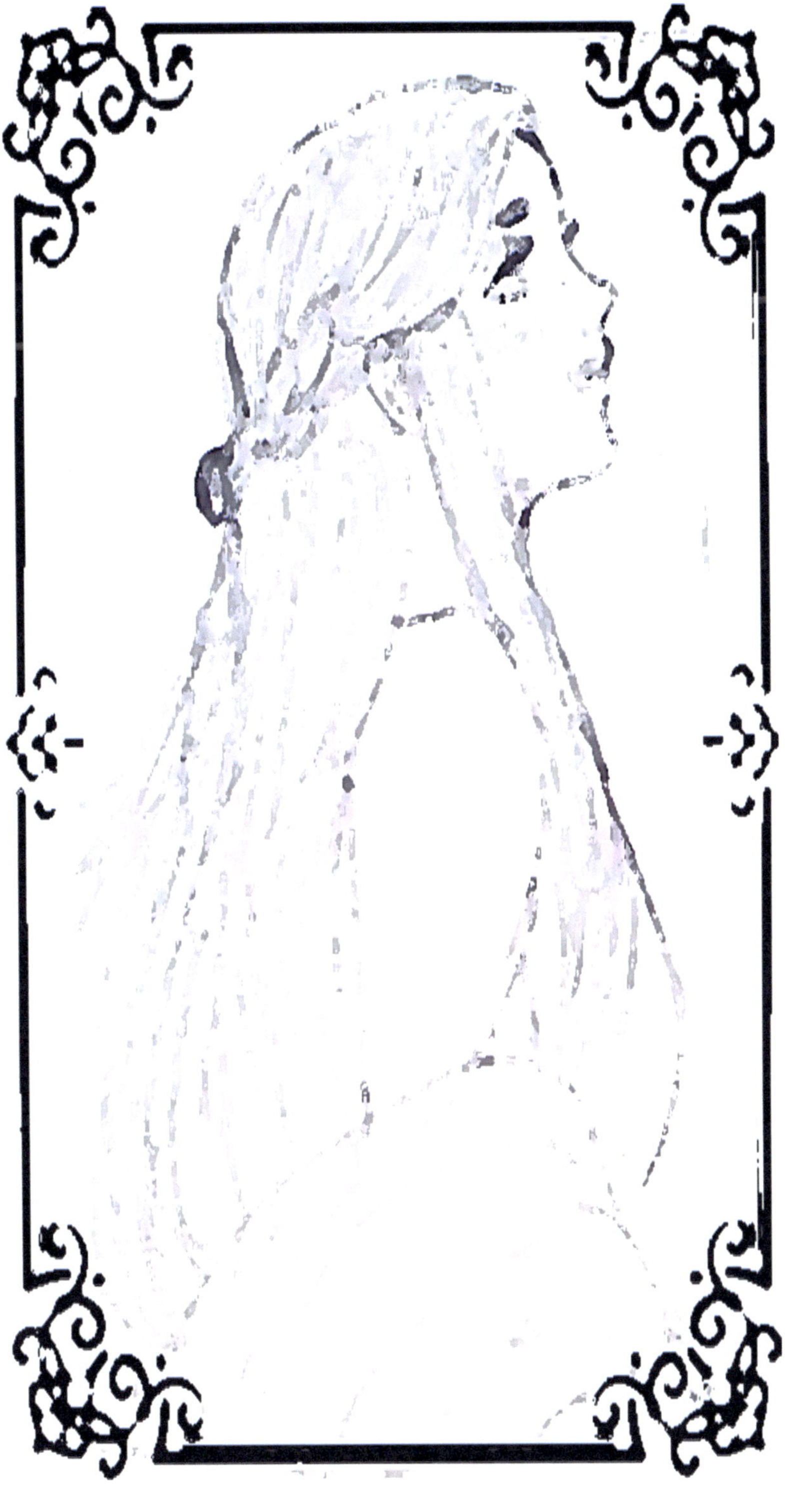

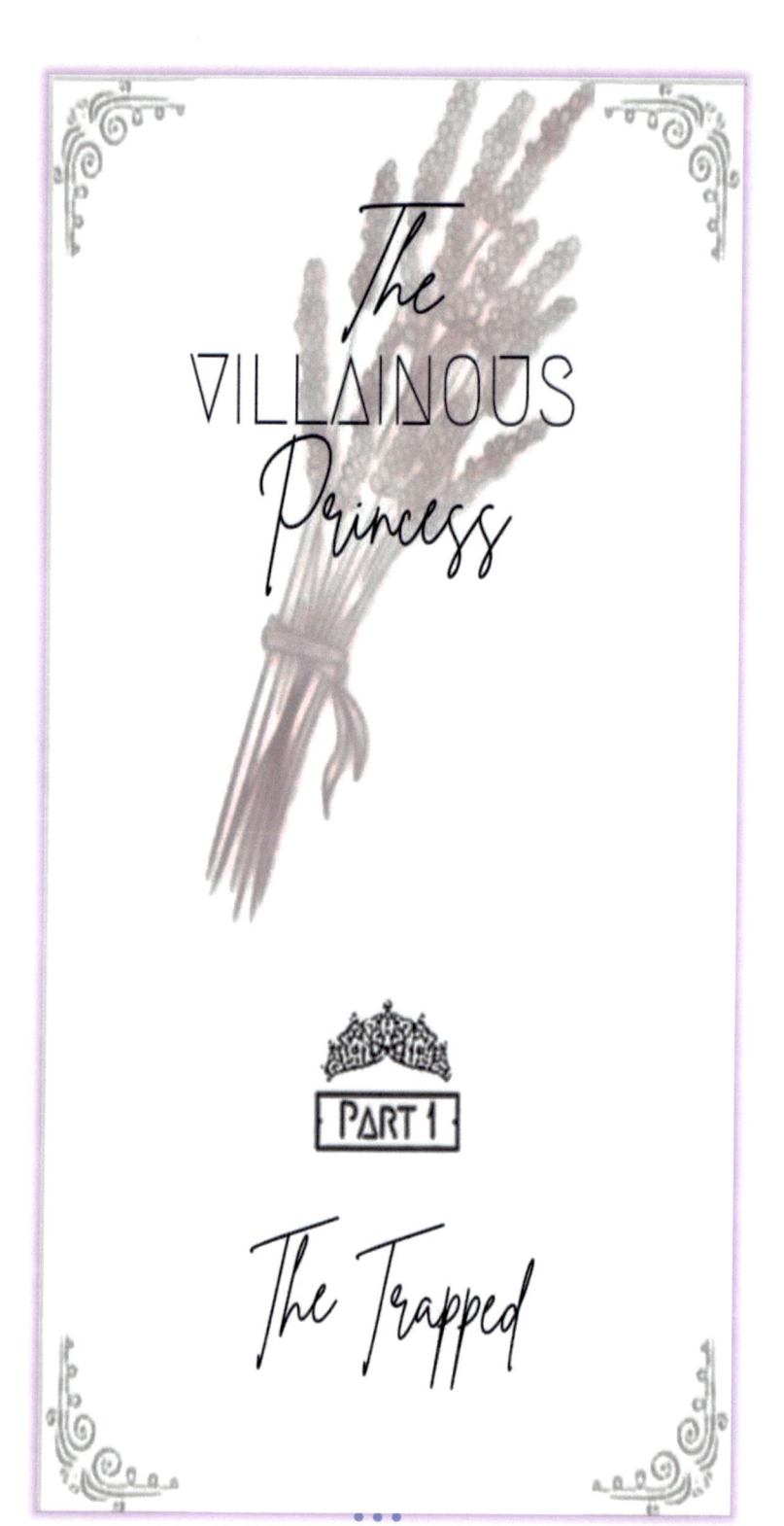

# The VILLAINOUS Princess

## PART 1

### The Trapped

# The Villainous Princess Muse Playlist

## (Alphabetical Order)

**Book 2.0 Theme: The Word Alive – Trapped**

1. Antti Martikainen - The March of the Templars
2. Billie Eilish – Ocean Eyes
3. Blue October – Into the Ocean
4. Breaking Benjamin – Follow me
5. Breaking Benjamin – Saturate
6. Citizen Soldier – Buried Alive
7. DIETER theme: Inferni – Two Steps from Hell
8. Disturbed – Forsaken
9. Disturbed – Stricken
10. Disturbed – You're Mine
11. Ellie Goulding – I know you care
12. Elly Duhé – Middle of the Night
13. Evanescence – Broken feat. Seether
14. Evanescence – Understanding
15. Evanescence – Weight of the world
16. Hilary Duff – Metamorphosis
17. In This Moment – Her Kiss
18. In This Moment – He said Eternity
19. JOHANNES theme: Sariel – Two Steps from Hell
20. KARMINDY theme: Silent Crying – Martin Czerny
21. Korn – Hold on
22. Linkin Park – Leave out all the rest

23. Marlene – Lavender Fields
24. Polyphia – Blood Bath
25. Our Last Night – Astronaut in the Ocean
26. Superchick – Beauty from pain
27. Superchick – Suddenly
28. Taylor Swift – Lavender Haze
29. The Devil Wears Prada – Trapped
30. Three Days Grace – On my own
31. WITCHZ – Drownin
32. Within Temptation – Pale

# The Villainous Princess

## Part 2

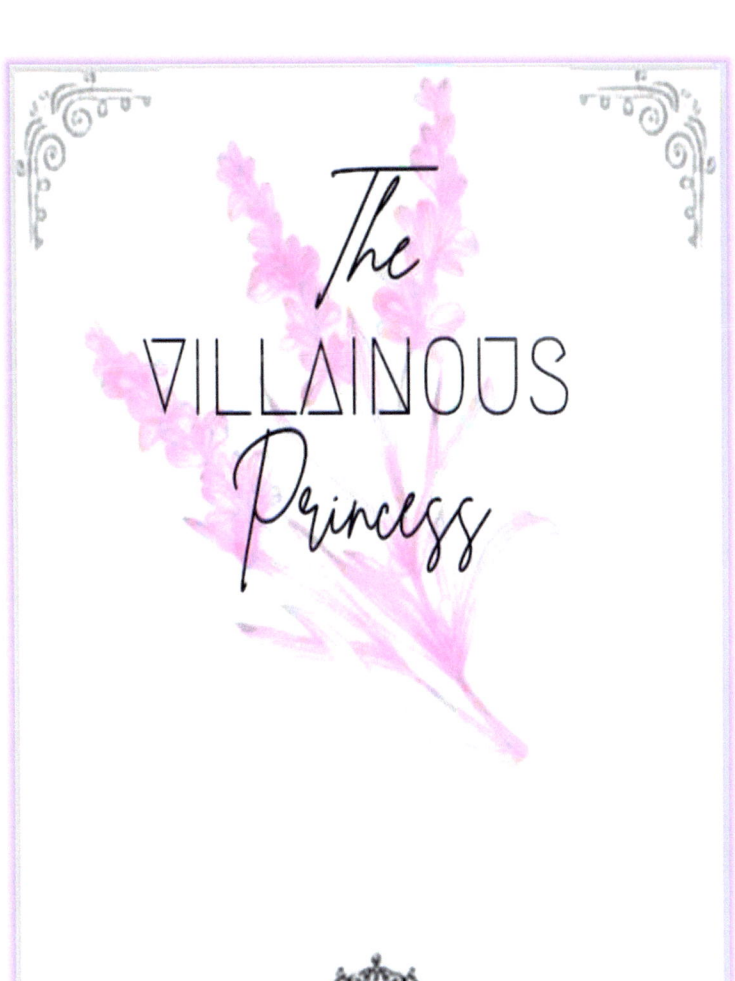

## The Freed

# The Villainous Princess Muse Playlist
## (Alphabetical Order)

**Book 2.5 Theme: Antti Martikainen - The March of the Templars**

1. Ariana Grande – Break Free
2. Britton – Liberated
3. Billie Eilish – Ocean Eyes
4. Blue October – Into the Ocean
5. Breaking Benjamin – Follow me
6. Breaking Benjamin – Saturate
7. Citizen Soldier – Buried Alive
33. DIETER theme: Inferni – Two Steps from Hell
8. Disturbed – Forsaken
9. Disturbed – Stricken
10. Disturbed – You're Mine
11. Ellie Goulding – I know you care
12. Elly Duhé – Middle of the Night
13. Eric Prydz – Liberate
14. Evanescence – Broken feat. Seether
15. Evanescence – Understanding
16. Evanescence – Weight of the world
17. Hilary Duff – Metamorphosis
18. In This Moment – Her Kiss
19. In This Moment – He said Eternity
34. JOHANNES theme: Sariel – Two Steps from Hell

35. KARMINDY theme: Silent Crying – Martin Czerny
20. Korn – Hold on
21. Linkin Park – Leave out all the rest
22. Marlene – Lavender Fields
23. Polyphia – Blood Bath
24. Our Last Night – Astronaut in the Ocean
25. Rage Against the Machine – Freedom
26. ROARY – Liberate
27. Superchick – Beauty from pain
28. Superchick – Suddenly
29. Taylor Swift – Lavender Haze
30. The Word Alive – Trapped
31. Three Days Grace – On my own
32. WITCHZ – Drownin
33. Within Temptation – Pale

# Family Tree - Karmindy
## Children

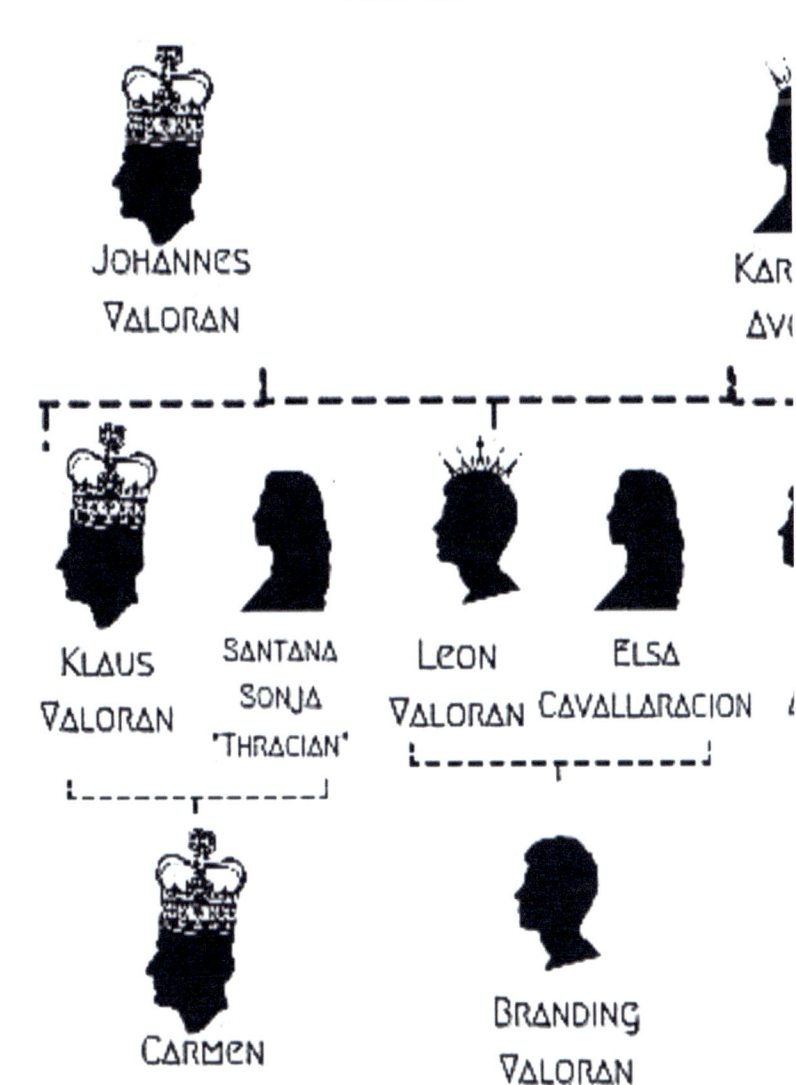

- Johannes Valoran
- Kar... Av...
  - Klaus Valoran
  - Santana Sonja "Thracian"
  - Leon Valoran
  - Elsa Cavallaracion
    - Carmen Valoran
    - Branding Valoran

# Family Tree - Karmindy
## Children

RMINDY /ELION — DIETER VON BOTH

KNOX AVELION | LINA VALORAN | CELINE VON BOTH | AMON FALICE

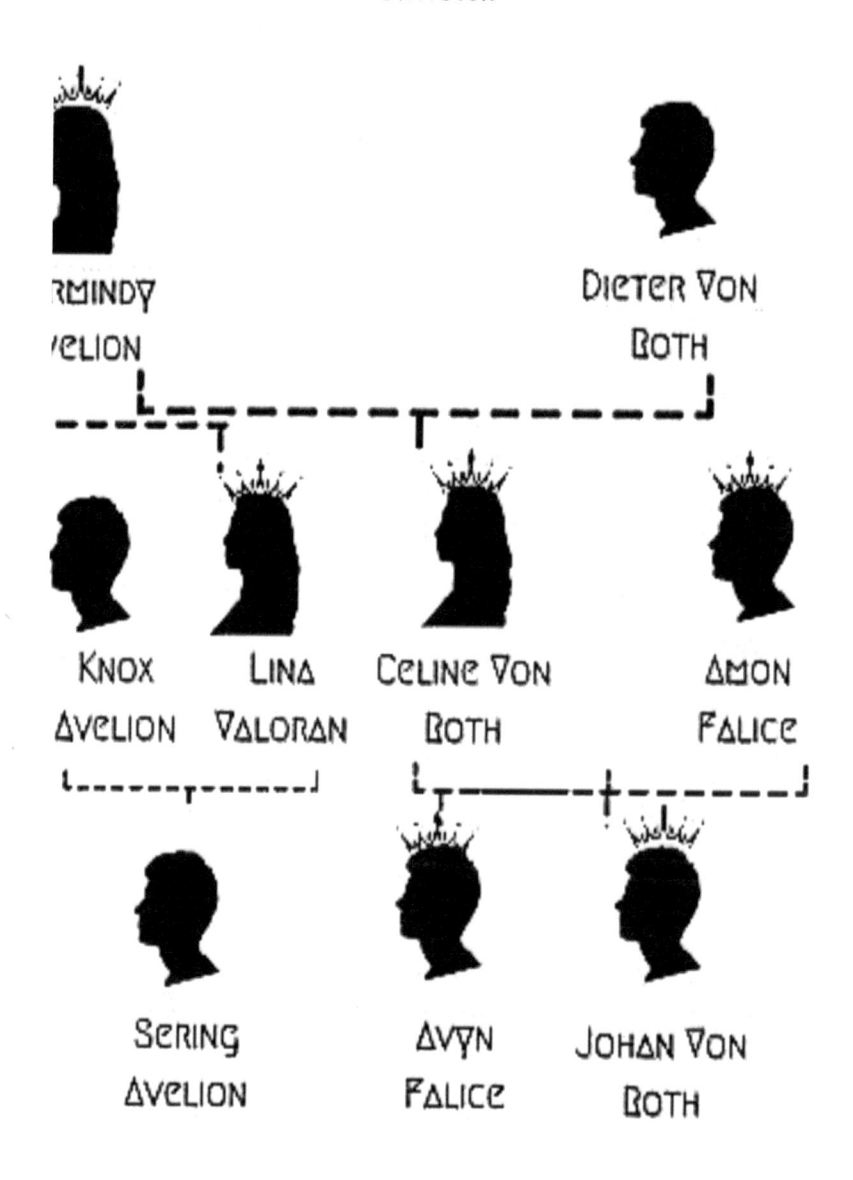

SERING AVELION | AVYN FALICE | JOHAN VON BOTH

# Character Profiles

## Karmindy

**Birthdate:** Folias's Blessing, 250 Central Imperial Year

**Faction:** Mage-Born

**Rankings:** Princess, Queen

**Stats Chart:**

| | | | | | | | | | |
|---|---|---|---|---|---|---|---|---|---|
| Mage Mana | ■ | | | | | | | | |
| Knight's Aura | ■ | | | | | | | | |
| Adaptability | ■ | ■ | ■ | ■ | ■ | | | | |
| Battle Skill | | | | | | | | | |
| Magic Ability | ■ | | | | | | | | |
| Intellect | ■ | ■ | ■ | ■ | | | | | |

# Character Art

## Realistic Art Character Inspiration

# Character Profiles

## Johannes

**Birthdate:** Veras's Height, 247 Central Imperial Year

**Faction:** Knight's Faction & Mage-Born

**Rankings:** Crowned Prince, King

**Stats Chart:**

|  | | | | | | | | | | |
|---|---|---|---|---|---|---|---|---|---|---|
| Mage Mana | ■ | ■ | ■ | ■ | ■ | | | | | |
| Knight's Aura | ■ | ■ | ■ | ■ | ■ | ■ | ■ | | | |
| Adaptability | ■ | ■ | ■ | ■ | ■ | ■ | ■ | ■ | ■ | |
| Battle Skill | ■ | ■ | ■ | ■ | ■ | ■ | ■ | ■ | ■ | |
| Magic Ability | ■ | ■ | ■ | | | | | | | |
| Intellect | ■ | ■ | ■ | ■ | ■ | ■ | ■ | ■ | | |

**Character Art**

# Realistic Art Character Inspiration

# Character Profiles

## Dieter

**Birthdate:** Nivis's End, 246 Central Imperial Year

**Faction:** Mage-Born

**Rankings:** Duke's son, Duke, Prince Consort

**Stats Chart:**

|  |  |
|---|---|
| Mage Mana | ▓▓▓▓▓▓░░░ |
| Knight's Aura | ▓▓▓▓▓▓▓░░ |
| Adaptability | ▓▓▓▓▓▓▓▓▓ |
| Battle Skill | ▓▓▓▓▓▓▓▓▓ |
| Magic Ability | ▓▓░░░░░░░ |
| Intellect | ▓▓▓▓▓▓▓▓▓ |

**Character Art**

## Realistic Art Character Inspiration

# Story Timeline

## 246 Central Imperial Year

**Nivis's End** – Dieter Von Roth is born

## 247 Central Imperial Year

**Veras's Height** – Johannes Valoran is born

## 250 Central Imperial Year

**Folias's Blessing** – Karmindy Avelion is born

## 265 Central Imperial Year

**Seed's Sewn** – Karmindy and Johannes married via proxy

**Veras's End** – Johannes returns from war

**Solaris's Reign** – Karmindy discovers pregnancy, Johannes called back to war

## 266 Central Imperial Year

**Seed's Sewn** – Klaus Valoran is born

## 270 Central Imperial Year

**Blizzard's Reign** – Dieter becomes Prince Consort

**Nivis's End** – Queen Dowager executed for assassination attempt of Karmindy

**Veras's End** – Celine Von Roth is born.

## 272 Central Imperial Year

**Folias's Blessing** – Leon and Lina Valoran are born.

## 275 Central Imperial Year

**Blizzard's Reign** – Karmindy miscarries

**Solaris's Gifts** – Karmindy passes away

## 287 Central Imperial Year

**Veras's End** – Klaus marries

## 288 Central Imperial Year

**Folias's Blessing** – Carmin Valoran is born

**Year's Fall** – Celine marries Amon Falice and moves overseas

## 549 Central Imperial Year

**Johannes Valoran IV signs Peace & Trade Treaty with Drakonians and Arch-Mage at the Mage's Tower and creates a new age, starting:**

001 Earth Drakonian Dynasty

## 021 Earth Drakonian Dynasty

War begins

## 149 Earth Drakonian Dynasty

Earth Drakonian rule overthrown,, creating 001 Fire Drakonian Dynasty

**MOVING INTO THE ROYAL'S SAGA BOOK 3**

**THE DISREGARDED DRAGON**

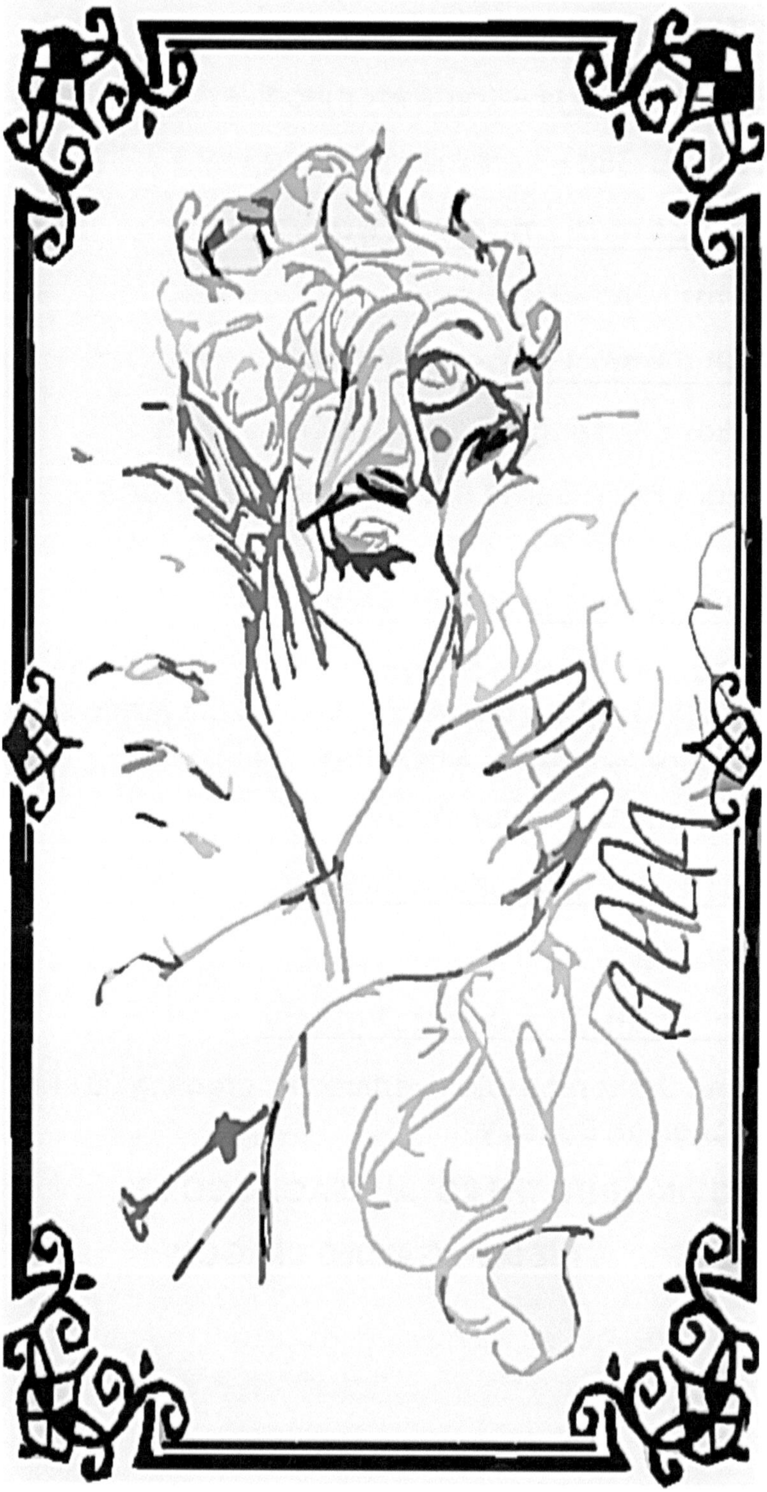

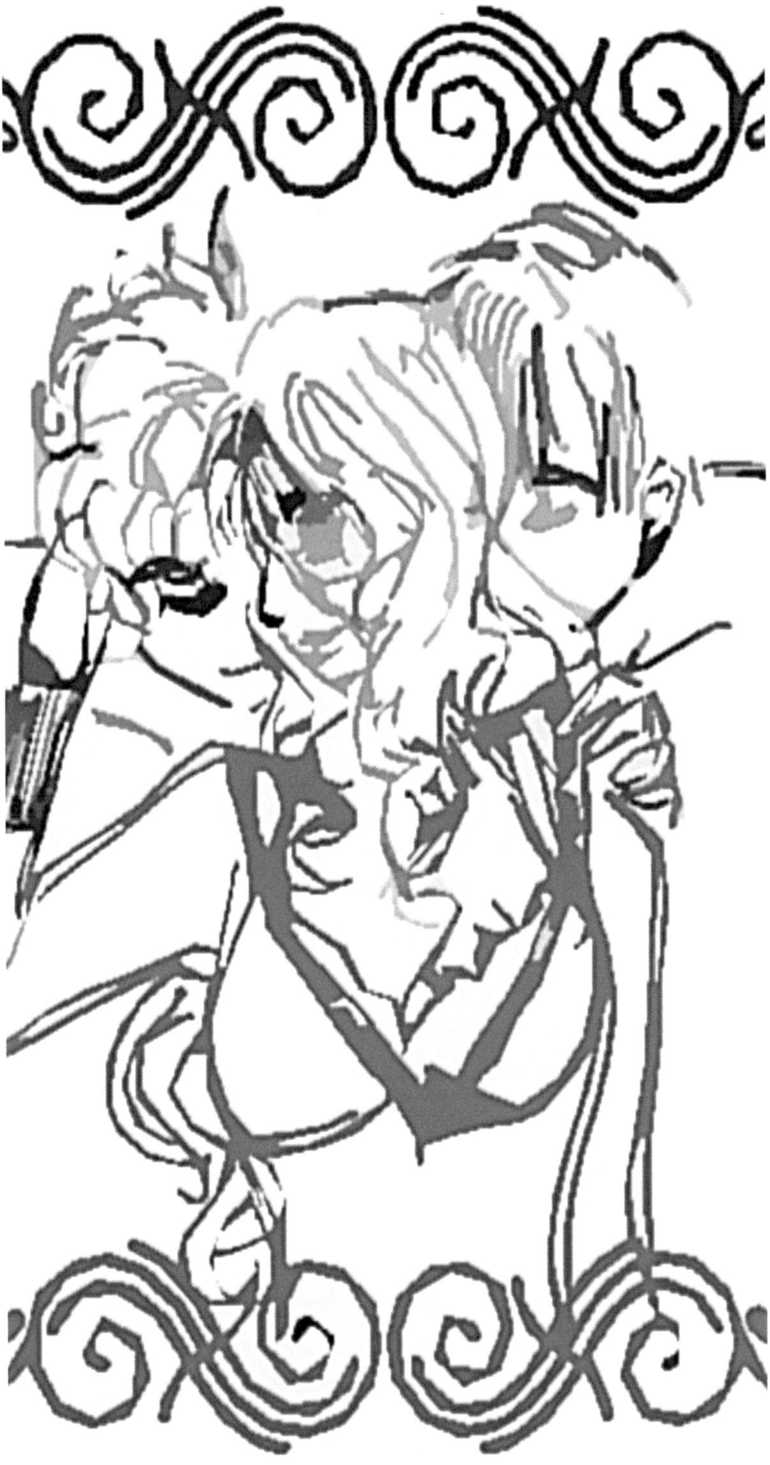

# The Disregarded Dragon

# The Disregarded Dragon Muse Playlist

## (Alphabetical Order)

### Book 3 Theme: Amanati – Femme Fatale

1. 2 Shadows – Fading from Misery
2. Citizen Soldier - Unbreakable
3. Disturbed – The Curse
4. Disturbed – Serpentine
5. Ellie Goulding – Burn
6. Ellie Goulding – My Blood
7. Imagine Dragons – Thunder
8. Jonathan Young – Dark Horse cover/Katy Perry mashup
9. Jonathan Young ft. Caleb Hyles – Whisper in the Dark cover
10. KAI theme: Warlord – Cavalera Conspiracy
11. Katy Perry – Firework
12. Korn – Coming Undone
13. Linkin Park – With You
14. Mint Fatigues – Snap Dragon
15. Nickleback – Savin' Me
16. NIEVES theme: Epic Hopeful - Proluxestudio
17. Nightwish – Astral Romance
18. Papa Roach – Gettin' away with murder
19. Skillet – Hero

20. SR-71 – Tomorrow
21. System of a Down – Aerials
22. System of a Down – I-E-A-I-A-I-O
23. System of a Down – Revenga
24. Two Steps from Hell – Dragonborn
25. Two Steps from Hell – Dragon
26. Two Steps from Hell – The Queen of the North
27. WITCHZ – The Wikked
28. Within Temptation – A Demon's Fate

# Family Tree

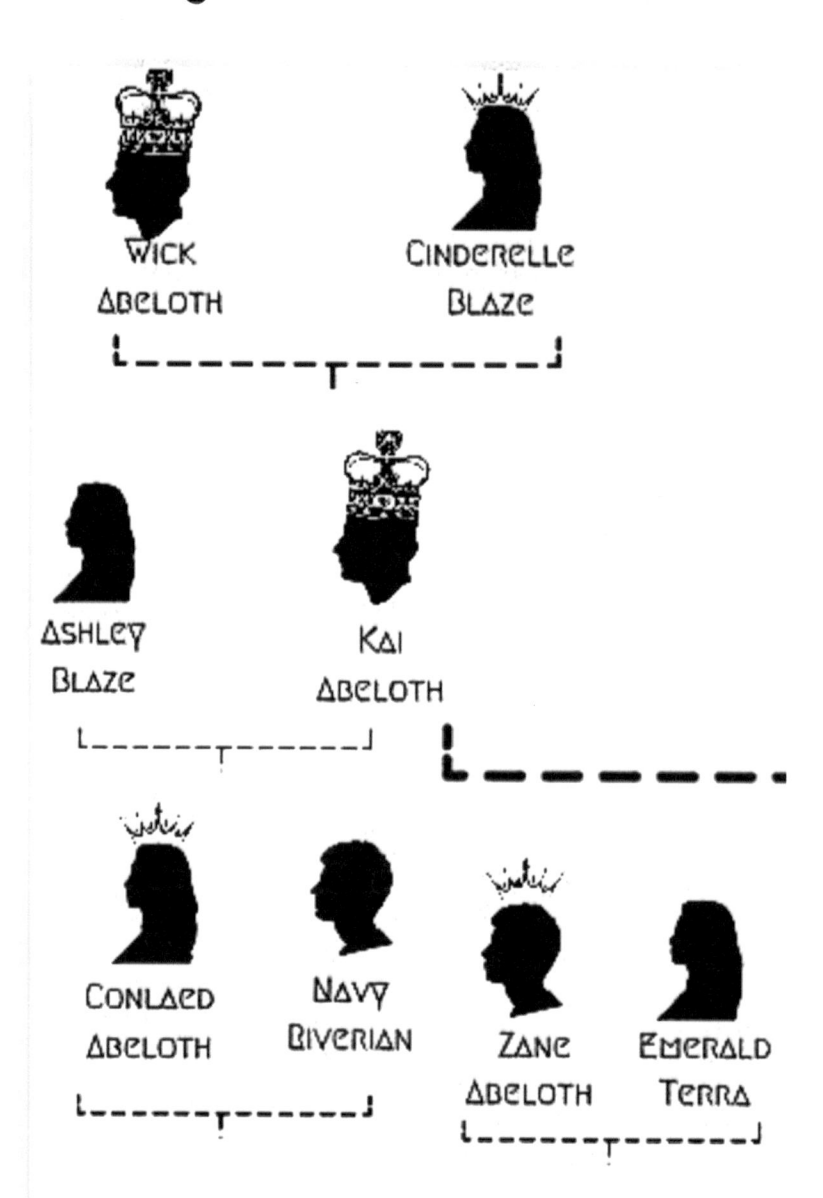

**Wick Abeloth** — **Cinderelle Blaze**

**Ashley Blaze** — **Kai Abeloth**

**Conlaed Abeloth** — **Navy Biverian**

**Zane Abeloth** — **Emerald Terra**

# Family Tree

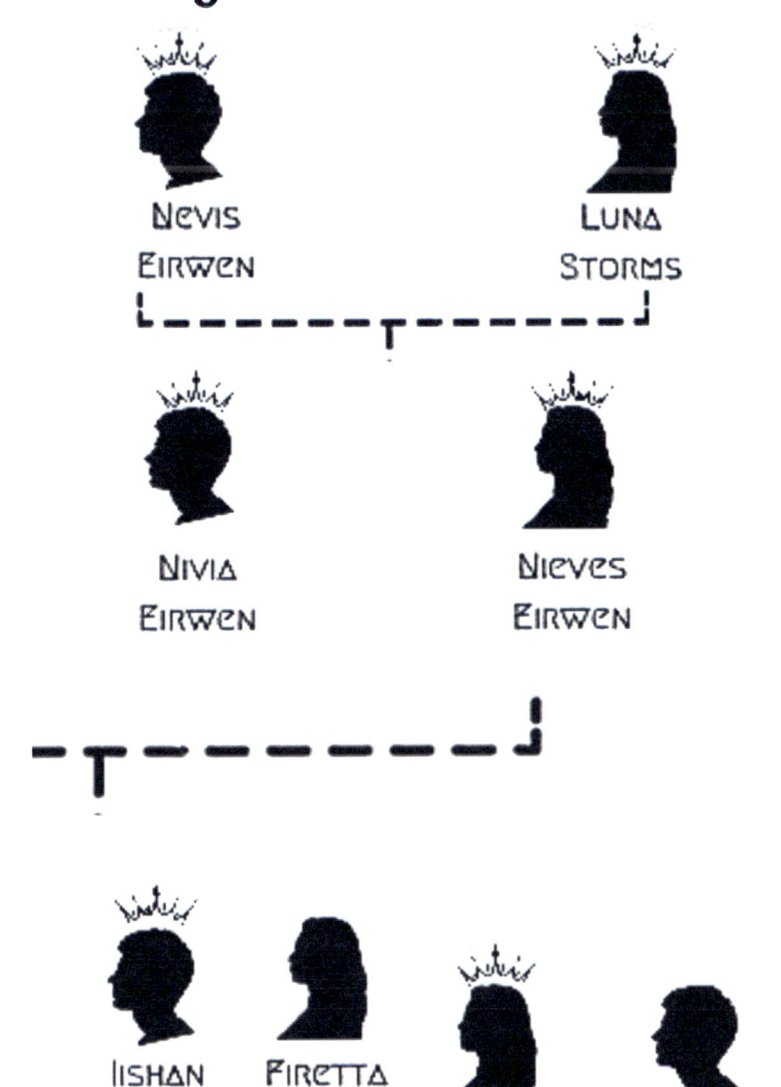

**Nevis Eirwen** — **Luna Storms**

**Nivia Eirwen**  **Nieves Eirwen**

**Iishan Abeloth** — **Firetta Sparks**   **Kiran Abeloth** — **Terrence Forge**

# Character Profiles

## Nieves

**Birthdate:** Solaris's Reign, 709 Fire Drakonian Dynasty

**Faction:** Mage-Born

**Rankings:** Princess, Empress

**Stats Chart:**

| | | | | | | | | |
|---|---|---|---|---|---|---|---|---|
| Mage Mana | | | | | | | | |
| Knight's Aura | | | | | | | | |
| Adaptability | | | | | | | | |
| Battle Skill | | | | | | | | |
| Magic Ability | | | | | | | | |
| Intellect | | | | | | | | |

## Character Art

# Realistic Art Character Inspiration

# Character Profiles
## Kai

**Birthdate:** Blizzard's Reign, 700 Fire Drakonian Dynasty

**Faction:** Knight's Faction & Mage-Born

**Rankings:** Crowned Prince, Emperor

**Stats Chart:**

| | | | | | | | | | |
|---|---|---|---|---|---|---|---|---|---|
| Mage Mana | ■ | ■ | ■ | ■ | ■ | ■ | ■ | | |
| Knight's Aura | ■ | ■ | ■ | ■ | ■ | ■ | ■ | ■ | ■ |
| Adaptability | ■ | ■ | | | | | | | |
| Battle Skill | ■ | ■ | ■ | ■ | ■ | ■ | ■ | ■ | ■ |
| Magic Ability | ■ | ■ | ■ | ■ | | | | | |
| Intellect | ■ | ■ | ■ | ■ | ■ | ■ | ■ | ■ | ■ |

## Character Art

## Realistic Art Character Inspiration

# *Story Timeline*

## 549 Central Imperial Year

Johannes Valoran IV signs Peace & Trade Treaty with Drakonians and Arch-Mage at the Mage's Tower and creates a new age, starting:

001 Earth Drakonian Dynasty

## 021 Earth Drakonian Dynasty

War begins

## 149 Earth Drakonian Dynasty

Earth Drakonian rule overthrown, creating:

001 Fire Drakonian Dynasty

## 700 Fire Drakonian Dynasty

**Blizzard's Reign** – Kai Abeloth is born

## 709 Fire Drakonian Dynasty

**Solaris's Reign** – Nieves Eirwen is born

## 722 Fire Drakonian Dynasty

**Blizzard's Reign** – Kai and Nieves marry

## 726 Fire Drakonian Dynasty

**Folias's Blessing** – Zane Abeloth is born

## 728 Fire Drakonian Dynasty

**Nivis's End** – Prince Ishaan and Princess Kiran Abeloth are born

## 732 Fire Drakonian Dynasty

**Veras's Height –** Princess Conlaed Abeloth marries Navy Riverian

## 737 Fire Drakonian Dynasty

**Solaris's Reign –** Conlaed's son is born

## 743 Fire Drakonian Dynasty

Zane marries General Sage's daughter, Emerald

## 746 Fire Drakonian Dynasty

Ishaan marries Firetta Sparks

## 747 Fire Drakonian Dynasty

Kiran marries Duke Terrence Forge

## 793 Fire Drakonian Dynasty

Kai passes away

## 798 Fire Drakonian Dynasty

Nieves passes away

## 997 Fire Drakonian Dynasty

**Drakonian age comes to an end, bringing in the era of the Dark and Light "Seer" sorcerers. Lawrence Dynasty 001 created**

**MOVING INTO THE ROYAL'S SAGA BOOK 4**

**THE HIDDEN QUEEN**

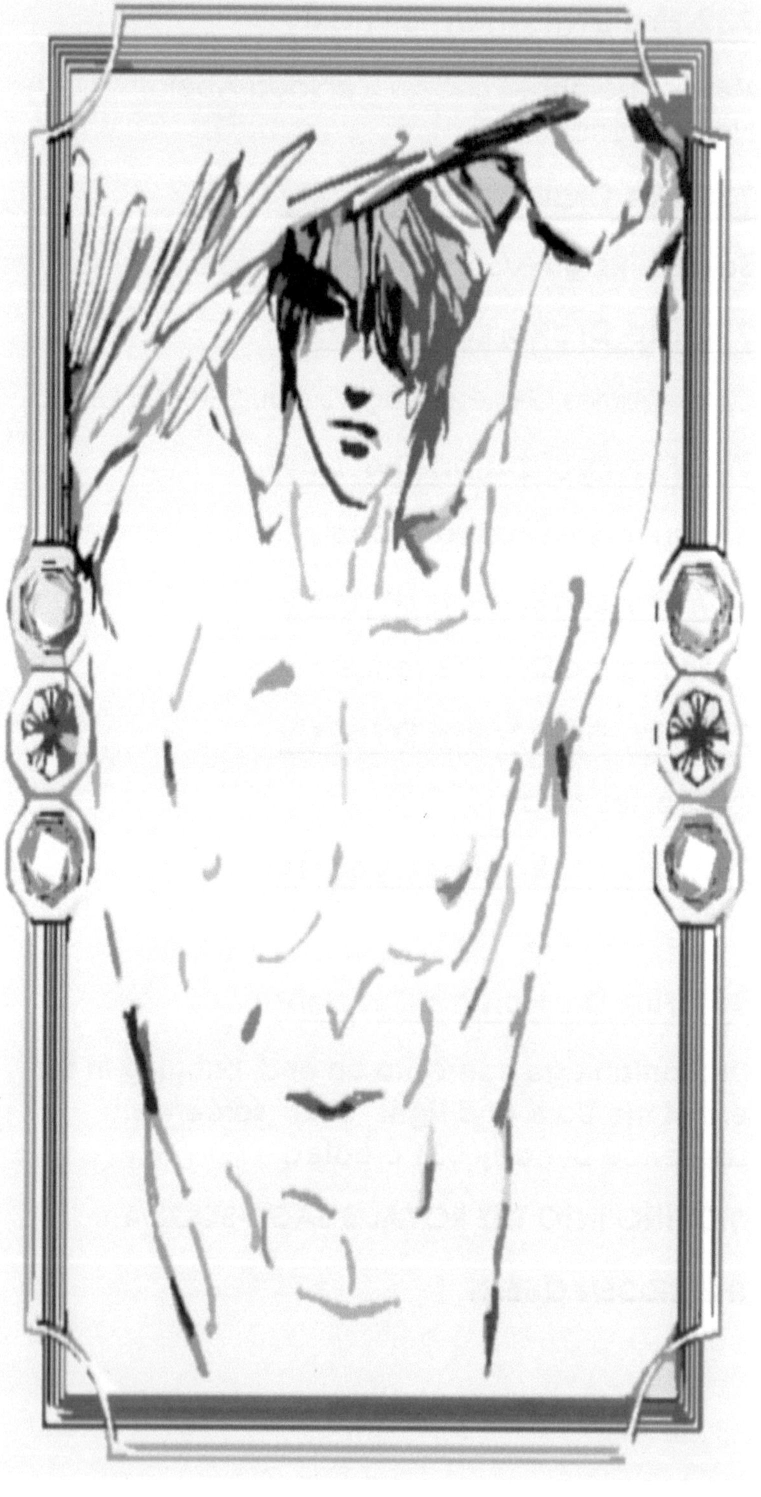

# The HIDDEN Queen

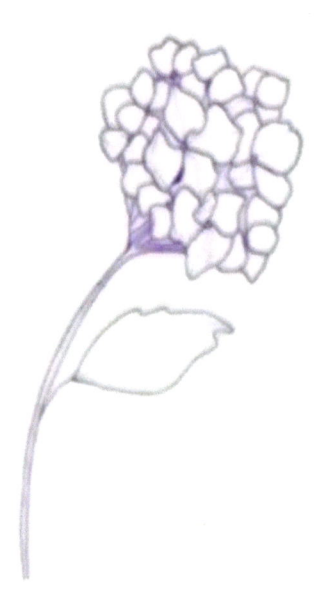

# The Hidden Queen Muse Playlist

*(Alphabetical Order)*

**Book 4 Theme: So Far Away – Staind**

1. 30 Seconds to Mars – I'll Attack
2. AFI – Kiss My Eyes and Lay Me To Sleep
3. Ashlynn Post – Silent Cries
4. Besomorph, Coopex, RIELL – Redemption
5. Breaking Benjamin – The Dark of You
6. Bring Me The Horizon – Throne
7. Camylio – Hurting me, hurting you
8. CARLISLE theme: The Show Must go On – 2Cellos
9. Citizen Soldier – Monster Made of Memories
10. David Guetta – Hey Mama
11. Evanescence – Imaginary
12. Evanescence – Taking Over Me
13. Fearless Soul – Find My Way
14. FesS – Sweet Dreams Cover
15. Fun – We Are Young '
16. Imagine Dragons - Enemy
17. Journey – Separate Ways
18. KINLEY theme: Butterflies (piano) – Tony Anderson
19. Lauren Paley – Hide and Seek cover
20. Maroon 5 – Sugar
21. MUDSPITTERS – Purple Hydrangeas
22. Nine Lashes – Anthem of the Lonely

23. Neoni – Darkside
24. Pink – Funhouse
25. Rex Mundi ft. Susana – Nothing At All
26. Rosse – coincidence (Slowed/reverb version by Sereine)
27. The Score – Stronger
28. WITCHZ – I'm Fine
29. YOHIO – My Nocturnal Serenade

# Family Tree

Carlisle Lawrence

Winter Lawrence

Cashmere Lawrence

# Family Tree

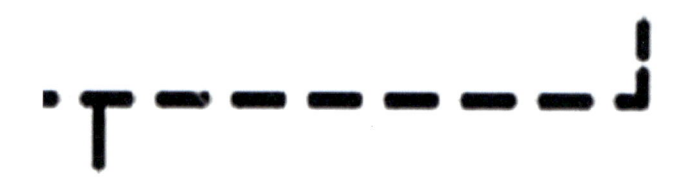

**Kinley Lawrence**

**Castiana Lawrence**

# Character Profiles

## Kinley

**Birthdate:** Year's Fall, 501 Lawrence Dynasty

**Faction:** Knight's Faction & Mage-Born

**Rankings:** Light Seer princess, Crowned Princess, Queen

**Stats Chart:**

| | | | | | | | | | | |
|---|---|---|---|---|---|---|---|---|---|---|
| Mage Mana | | | | | | | | | | |
| Knight's Aura | | | | | | | | | | |
| Adaptability | | | | | | | | | | |
| Battle Skill | | | | | | | | | | |
| Magic Ability | | | | | | | | | | |
| Intellect | | | | | | | | | | |

**Character Art**

## Realistic Art Character Inspiration

# Character Profiles

## Johannes

**Birthdate:** Year's Fall, 500 Lawrence Dynasty

**Faction:** Knight's Faction & Mage-Born

**Rankings:** Dark Seer Crowned Prince, King

**Stats Chart:**

|  | | | | | | | | | |
|---|---|---|---|---|---|---|---|---|---|
| Mage Mana | ■ | ■ | ■ | ■ | ■ | | | | |
| Knight's Aura | ■ | ■ | ■ | ■ | ■ | ■ | ■ | | |
| Adaptability | ■ | ■ | | | | | | | |
| Battle Skill | ■ | ■ | ■ | ■ | ■ | | | | |
| Magic Ability | ■ | ■ | | | | | | | |
| Intellect | ■ | ■ | ■ | ■ | ■ | ■ | | | |

# Character Art

# Realistic Art Character Inspiration

# Story Timeline

## 997 Fire Drakonian Dynasty

Drakonian age comes to an end, bringing in the era of the Dark and Light "Seer" sorcerers. Lawrence Dynasty 001 created

## 500 Lawrence Dynasty

**Year's Fall –** Dark Seer Prince Carlisle Lawrence is born

## 501 Lawrence Dynasty

**Year's Fall –** Light Seer Princess is born, given to knight to run away with

## 502 Lawrence Dynasty

**Blizzard's Reign –** Lawrence family begins search for the lost and hidden princess

## 509 Lawrence Dynasty

**Nivis's End –** Kinley rescued, brought to Carlisle, named "Kinley," Carlisle and Kinley married

## 517 Lawrence Dynasty

**Year's Fall –** Kinley catches Carlisle cheating on her

## 519 Lawrence Dynasty

**Year's Fall –** Kinley saves Carlisle from getting stabbed

## 520 Lawrence Dynasty

**Moon's Dance** – Carlisle and Kinley have their first night

**Year's Fall** – Kinley kidnapped by her parents,

## 521 Lawrence Dynasty

**Blizzard's Reign** – Carlisle rescues Kinley

**Solaris's Reign** – Winter Lawrence is born

## 529 Lawrence Dynasty

Princess Cashmere and Dark Seer Princess Castiana are born, Castiana sent to the Southern kingdom

## 665 Lawrence Dynasty

Lawrence Dynasty falls when Seer Queen attacks her Seer King, he signs deal with sorcerers and installs a new system, creating the "Matrimony Seal" system and giving families special magical abilities. Creating Imperial Lunar Year 001.

**MOVING TO THE ROYAL'S SAGA BOOK 5**

**THE CONQUERING EMPRESS**

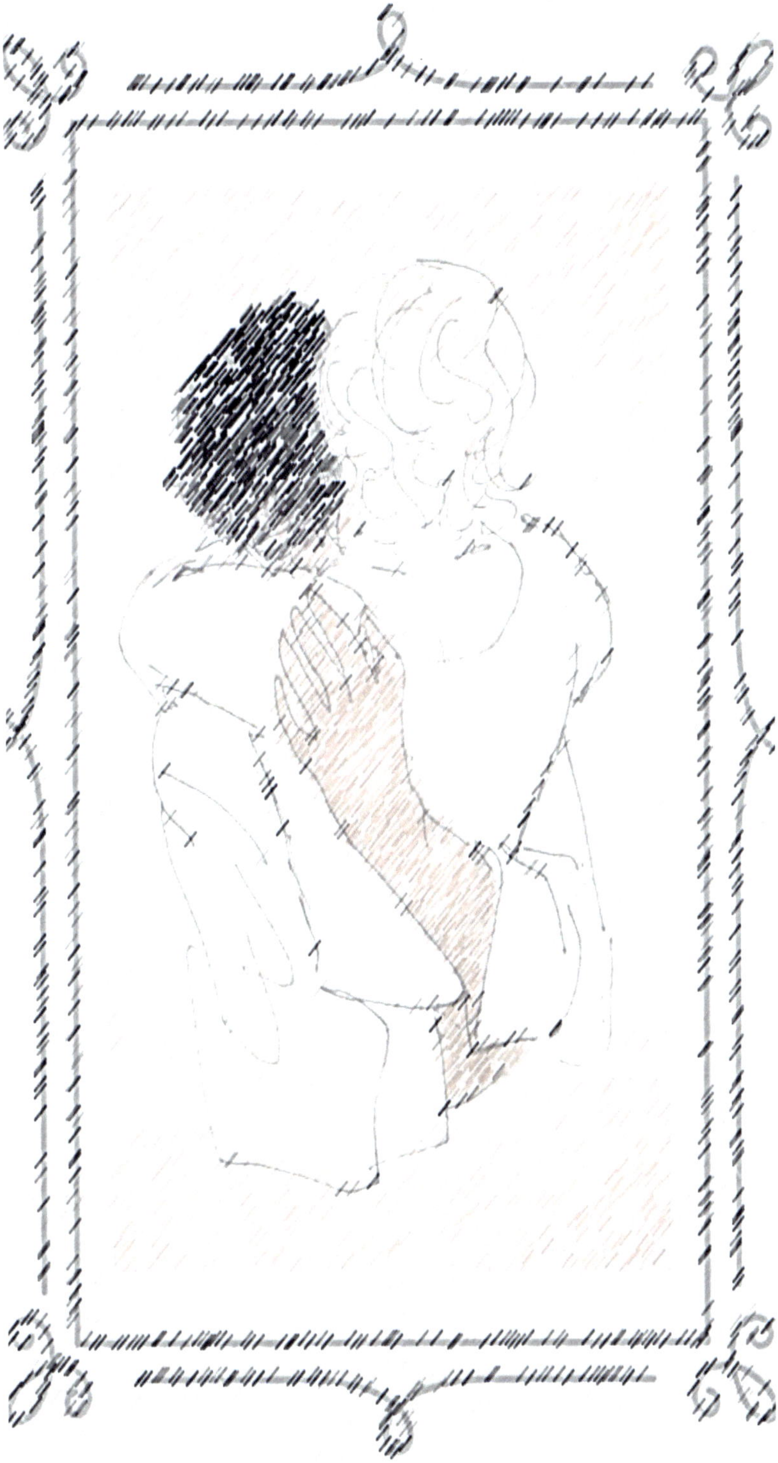

# The Conquering Empress

# The Conquering Empress Muse Playlist
## (Alphabetical Order)

**Book 5 Theme: Ellie Goulding – Hollow Crown**

### Muse Playlist (Alphabetical Order)

1. Alicia Keys – Daffodils
2. Billy Squier – All Night Long
3. Billy Squier – In the Dark
4. Breaking Benjamin – Firefly
5. Breaking Benjamin – Polyamorous
6. Christina Aguilera – Fighter
7. Citizen Soldier – Weight of the World
8. Corey Hart – Sunglasses at Night
9. Ellie Goulding – Lights
10. Eminem – Go to Sleep
11. Emmy Meli – I AM WOMAN
12. Florence + The Machine – Daffodil
13. Imagine Dragons – Thunder
14. Jonathan Young – Every time we Touch Popfunk cover
15. Julie Anna – Shine Bright like a Diamond
16. JVKE – Golden Hour
17. KATRIA theme: Vangelus – Light and Shadow
18. Meghan Trainor – Badass Woman
19. Nightcore – Fallen

20. Nightwish – Last Ride of the Day
21. Paramore – CrushCrushCrush
22. Sia – Unstoppable (sped up + slowed version)
23. Shakira – Loca
24. Skillet – Whispers in the Dark
25. Staind – Now
26. System of a Down – Psycho
27. Taylor Swift – Bejeweled
28. The Cardigans – Lovefool
29. The Red Jumpsuit Apparatus – Face Down
30. Three Day's Grace – It's All Over
31. Two Steps from Hell – Rise Above
32. VIOREL theme: Peter Dundry – Daughters of Darkness
**33.** Xavier Rudd – Follow the Sun

# Family Tree

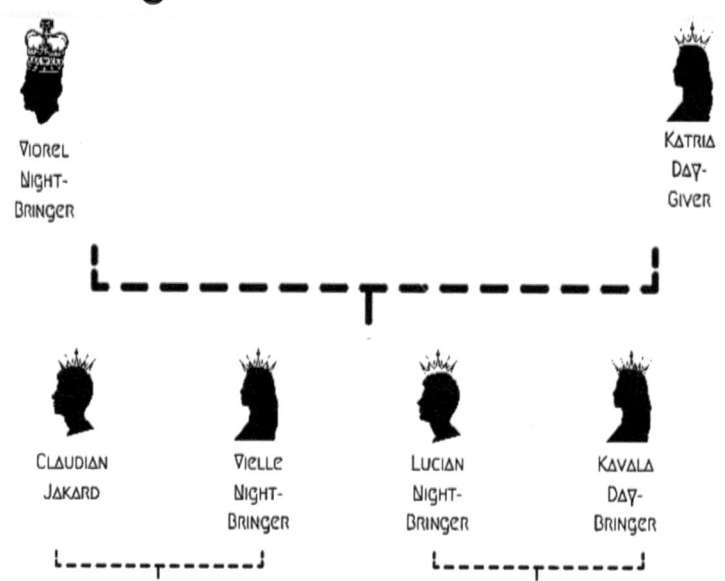

**Viorel Night-Bringer** — **Katria Day-Giver**

- Claudian Jakard
- Vielle Night-Bringer
- Lucian Night-Bringer
- Kavala Day-Bringer

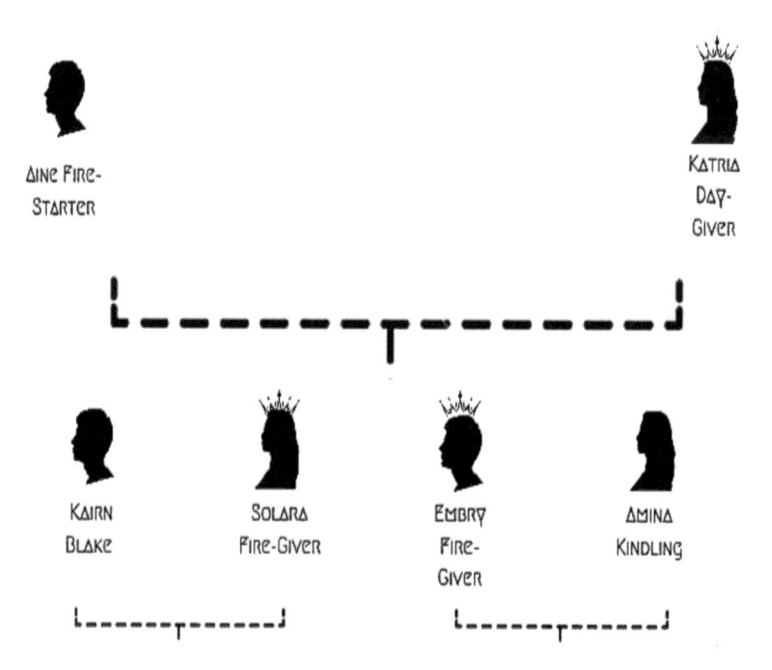

**Aine Fire-Starter** — **Katria Day-Giver**

- Kairn Blake
- Solara Fire-Giver
- Embry Fire-Giver
- Amina Kindling

106

# Family Tree

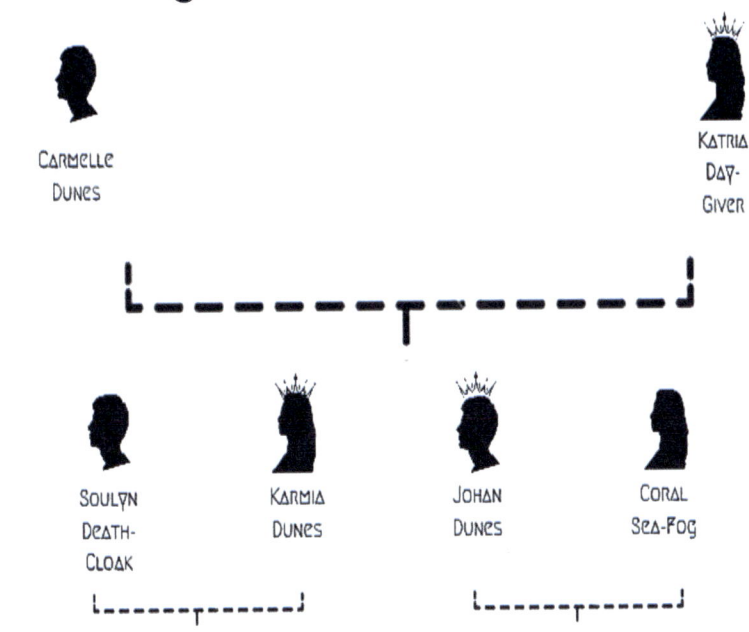

Carmelle Dunes — Katria Day-Giver

Soulyn Death-Cloak — Karmia Dunes    Johan Dunes — Coral Sea-Fog

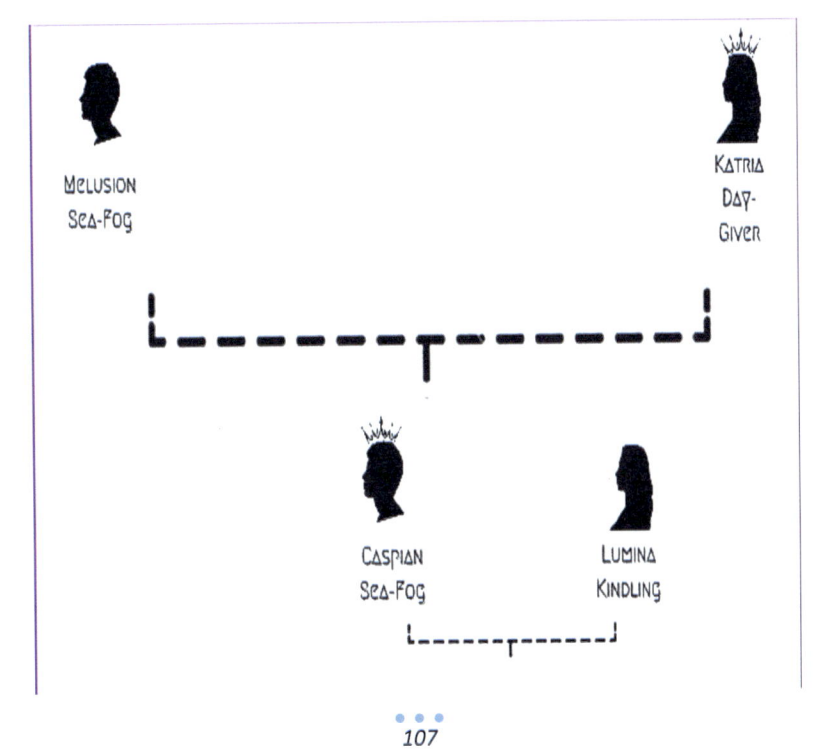

Melusion Sea-Fog — Katria Day-Giver

Caspian Sea-Fog — Lumina Kindling

# Character Profiles
## Katria

**Birthdate:** Solaris's Reign, 777 Imperial Lunar Year

**Faction:** Mage-Born

**Rankings:** Day-Giver princess, Crowned Princess, Day-Giver Empress

**Stats Chart:**

|  | | | | | | | | | |
|---|---|---|---|---|---|---|---|---|---|
| Mage Mana | ■ | ■ | ■ | ■ | ■ | ■ | ■ | | |
| Knight's Aura | | | | | | | | | |
| Adaptability | ■ | ■ | ■ | | | | | | |
| Battle Skill | | | | | | | | | |
| Magic Ability | ■ | ■ | ■ | ■ | ■ | ■ | ■ | ■ | ■ |
| Intellect | ■ | ■ | ■ | ■ | ■ | ■ | | | |

## Character Art

# Realistic Art Character Inspiration

# Character Profiles
## Viorel

**Birthdate:** Moon's Dance, 771 Imperial Lunar Year

**Faction:** Knight Faction & Mage-Born

**Rankings:** Night-Bringer Crowned Prince, Night-Bringer emperor

**Stats Chart**

|  |  |
|---|---|
| Mage Mana | █████████░ |
| Knight's Aura | ████████░░ |
| Adaptability | ██████░░░░ |
| Battle Skill | ███████░░░ |
| Magic Ability | ██████████ |
| Intellect | █████████░ |

# Character Art

## Realistic Art Character Inspiration

# Character Profiles

## Aine

**Birthdate:** Solaris's Gifts, 775 Imperial Lunar Year

**Faction:** Knight's Faction & Mage-Born

**Rankings:** Marquess's 4th son, Consort, Chief Consort, Prince Consort, King Consort

**Stats Chart**

| | | | | | | | | | |
|---|---|---|---|---|---|---|---|---|---|
| **Mage Mana** | | | | | | | | | |
| **Knight's Aura** | | | | | | | | | |
| **Adaptability** | | | | | | | | | |
| **Battle Skill** | | | | | | | | | |
| **Magic Ability** | | | | | | | | | |
| **Intellect** | | | | | | | | | |

## Character Art

# Realistic Art Character Inspiration

# Character Profiles

## Melusion

**Birthdate:** Seed's Sewn, 778 Imperial Lunar Year

**Faction:** Mage-Born

**Rankings:** Marquess's son, Consort, Prince Consort, King Consort

**Stats Chart**

| | | | | | | | | | |
|---|---|---|---|---|---|---|---|---|---|
| Mage Mana | ■ | ■ | ■ | ■ | ■ | | | | |
| Knight's Aura | | | | | | | | | |
| Adaptability | ■ | ■ | ■ | ■ | ■ | ■ | | | |
| Battle Skill | ■ | | | | | | | | |
| Magic Ability | ■ | ■ | ■ | ■ | | | | | |
| Intellect | ■ | ■ | ■ | ■ | ■ | ■ | | | |

# Character Art

## Realistic Art Character Inspiration

# Character Profiles

## Carmelle

**Birthdate:** Veras's Height, 774 Imperial Lunar Year

**Faction:** Knight's Faction

**Rankings:** Knight Captain, named Count, named Marquess, Consort, Prince Consort, King Consort

**Stats Chart**

|  |  |
|---|---|
| Mage Mana | 0 |
| Knight's Aura | 9 |
| Adaptability | 8 |
| Battle Skill | 9 |
| Magic Ability | 0 |
| Intellect | 8 |

## Character Art

# Realistic Art Character Inspiration

# Story Timeline

## 665 Lawrence Dynasty

Lawrence Dynasty falls when Seer Queen attacks her Seer King, he signs deal with sorcerers and installs a new system, creating the "Matrimony Seal" system and giving families special magical abilities. Creating Imperial Lunar Year 001

## 771 Imperial Lunar Year

**Moon's Dance** – Viorel Night-Bringer is born.

## 774 Imperial Lunar Year

**Veras's Height** – Carmelle Dunes is born

## 775 Imperial Lunar Year

**Solaris's Gifts** – Aine Fire-Starter is born

## 777 Imperial Lunar Year

**Solaris's Reign** – Katria Day-Giver is born

## 778 Imperial Lunar Year

**Seed's Sewn** – Melusion Sea-Fog is born

## 790 Imperial Lunar Year

**Moon's Dance** – Viorel and Katria marry

## 792 Imperial Lunar Year

**Veras's End** – Vielle Night-Bringer is born

## 795 Imperial Lunar Year

**Veras's Height** – Katria brings in Aine as Consort

## 796 Imperial Lunar Year

**Veras's Height** – Solara Fire-Giver is born

## 798 Imperial Lunar Year

Embry Fire-Giver is born

## 802 Imperial Lunar Year

Caspian Sea-Fog is born

## 808 Imperial Lunar Year

Lucian Night-Bringer is born

## 811 Imperial Lunar Year

Johan and Karmia Dunes are born

## 813 Imperial Lunar Year

Vielle Night-Bringer marries Claudian Jakard

## 822 Imperial Lunar Year

Lucian Night-Bringer marries Kavala Day-Giver

**MOVING TO THE ROYAL'S SAGA BOOK 6**

### THE ABANDONED PRINCE

**The Abandoned Prince operates on a different calendar system! Introducing Imperial Year**

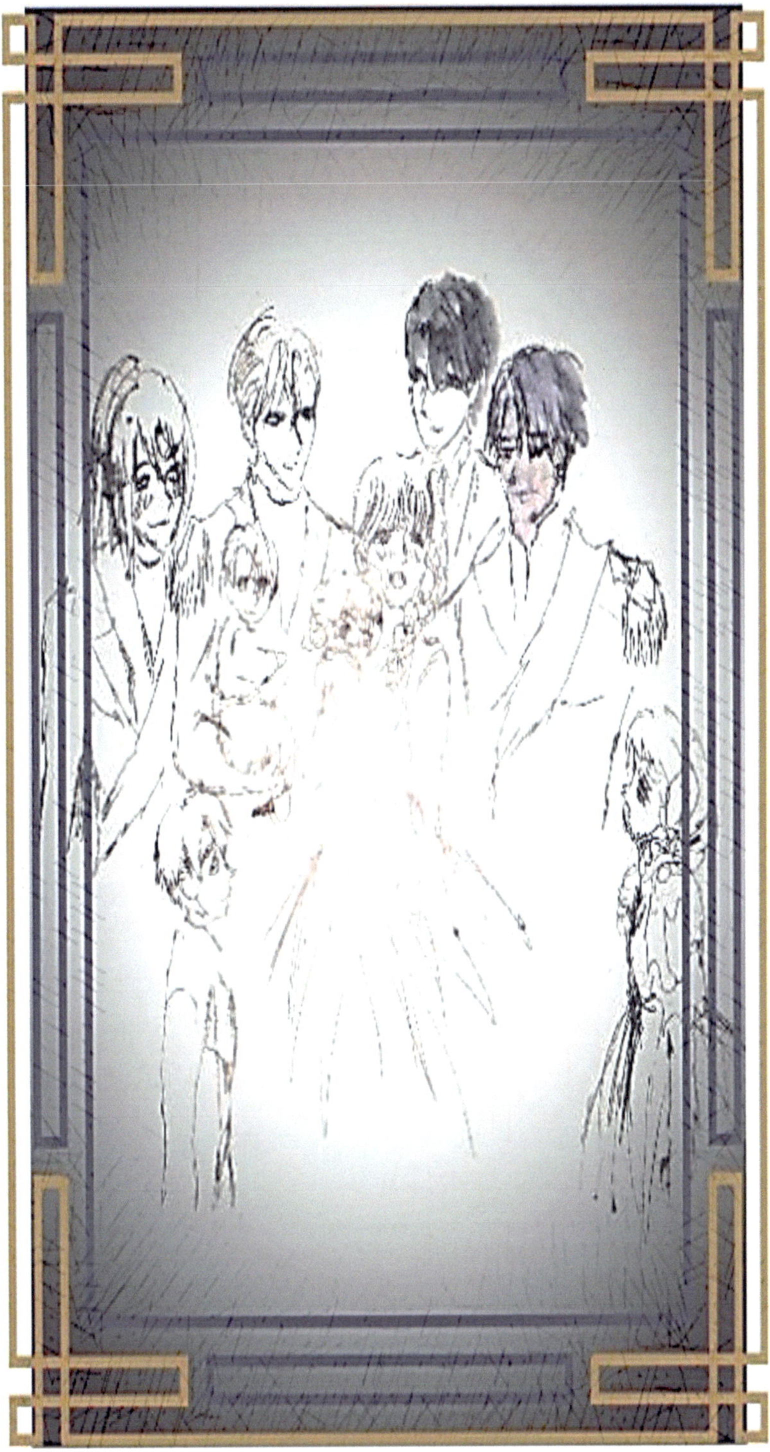

# The Abandoned Prince

# The Abandoned Prince Muse Playlist

*(Alphabetical Order)*

**Book 6 Theme: Ricky Rich, Dardan – Habibi (Slowed and Reverb version)**

1. Abdul Al Kahabir – Arabian Desert
2. Ancient Egyptian Music – Bastet
3. Ancient Egyptian Music – Pharoah Ramses II
4. Apocalyptica ft. Brent Smith – Not Strong Enough
5. Asaya (Original Remix)
6. Breaking Benjamin – The Dark of You
7. Citizen Soldier – Death of Me
8. Clean Bandit ft. Sean Paul & Anne-Marie – Rockabye
9. CLAUDIANNE theme: Meditation Music Zone – White Lotus Flower
10. Crystofinsomnia Cinematic – Dark Magicians
11. Dark Egyptian Music – Anubis
12. Doja Cat – Woman
13. Elley Duhe – Middle of the Night (Slowed & Reverb version)
14. Epic Egyptian Music – Apophis
15. IVOXYGEN – Abandoned
16. Jonathan Young – Arabian Nights
17. Kays Beats – Desert Rose
18. KLAUS theme: Smashtrax – Prince of Persian
19. Maneskin – Beggin

20. Monoir & Dharia – Incredible (Slowed & Reverb version)
21. Poison – Every Rose has its Thorn
22. Rex Mundi ft. Susana – Nothing at All
23. Rod Wave – Abandoned
24. Royalty Free Music Background – Arabian Dance
25. SAINt JHN – Roses
26. Sam Tinnesz – Play with Fire (Slowed & Reverb version)
27. Seal – Kiss from a Rose
28. Separate Ways – Journey
29. Skrillex & Damian Jr. Gong Marley – Make it Bun Dem
30. Spice, Sean Paul & Shaggy – Go Down Deh
31. Sufi Lounge – Desert Secrets
32. The Arabian Night – Instrumental Belly Dance music
33. Zwirek – Arabian Nights

# Family Tree

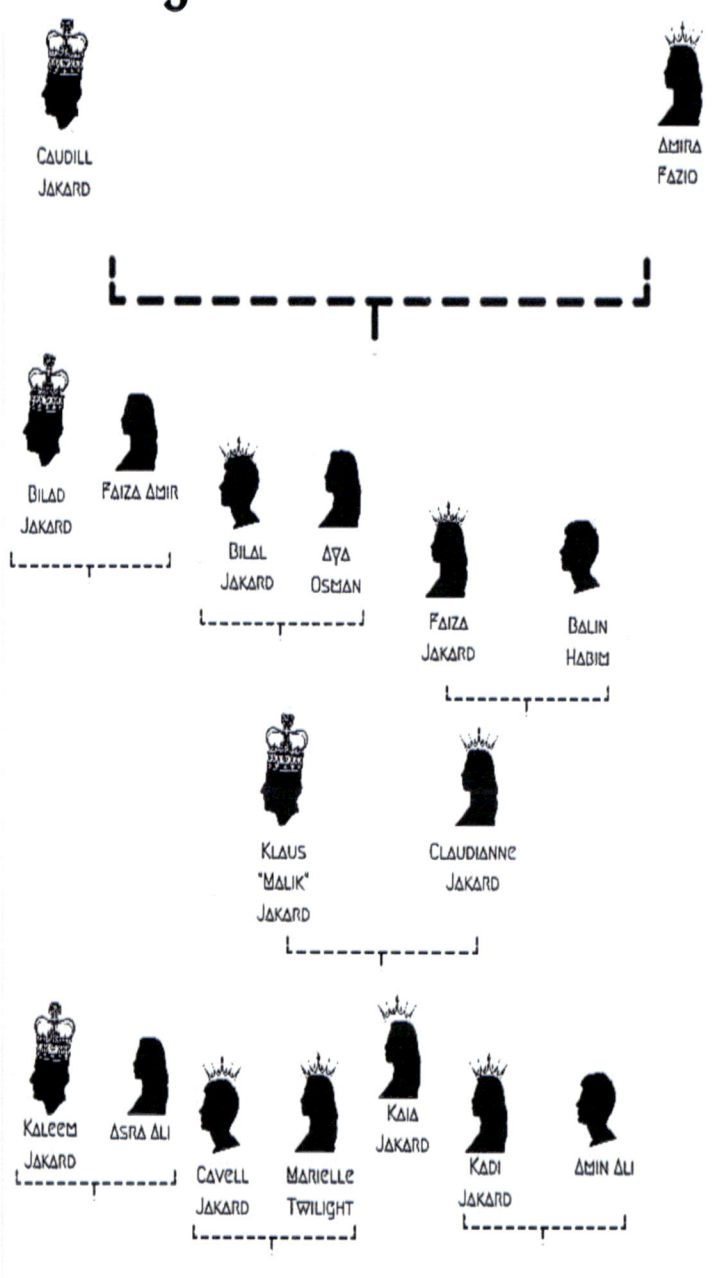

- Caudill Jakard — Amira Fazio
  - Bilad Jakard — Faiza Amir
  - Bilal Jakard — Aya Osman
  - Faiza Jakard — Balin Habim
    - Klaus "Malik" Jakard — Claudianne Jakard
      - Kaleem Jakard — Asra Ali
      - Cavell Jakard — Marielle Twilight
      - Kaia Jakard
      - Kadi Jakard — Amin Ali

# Map

## Jakard Kingdom

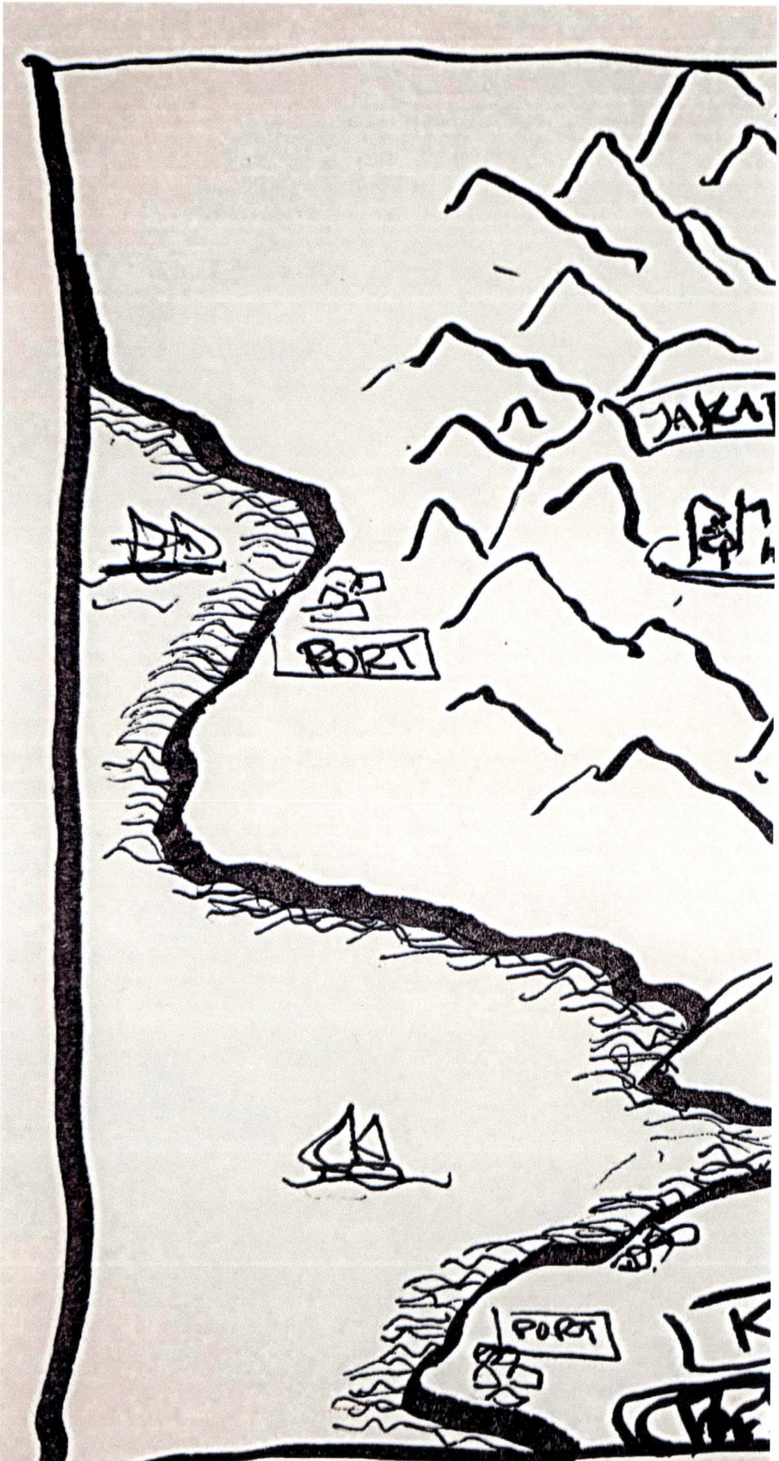
PORT
PORT

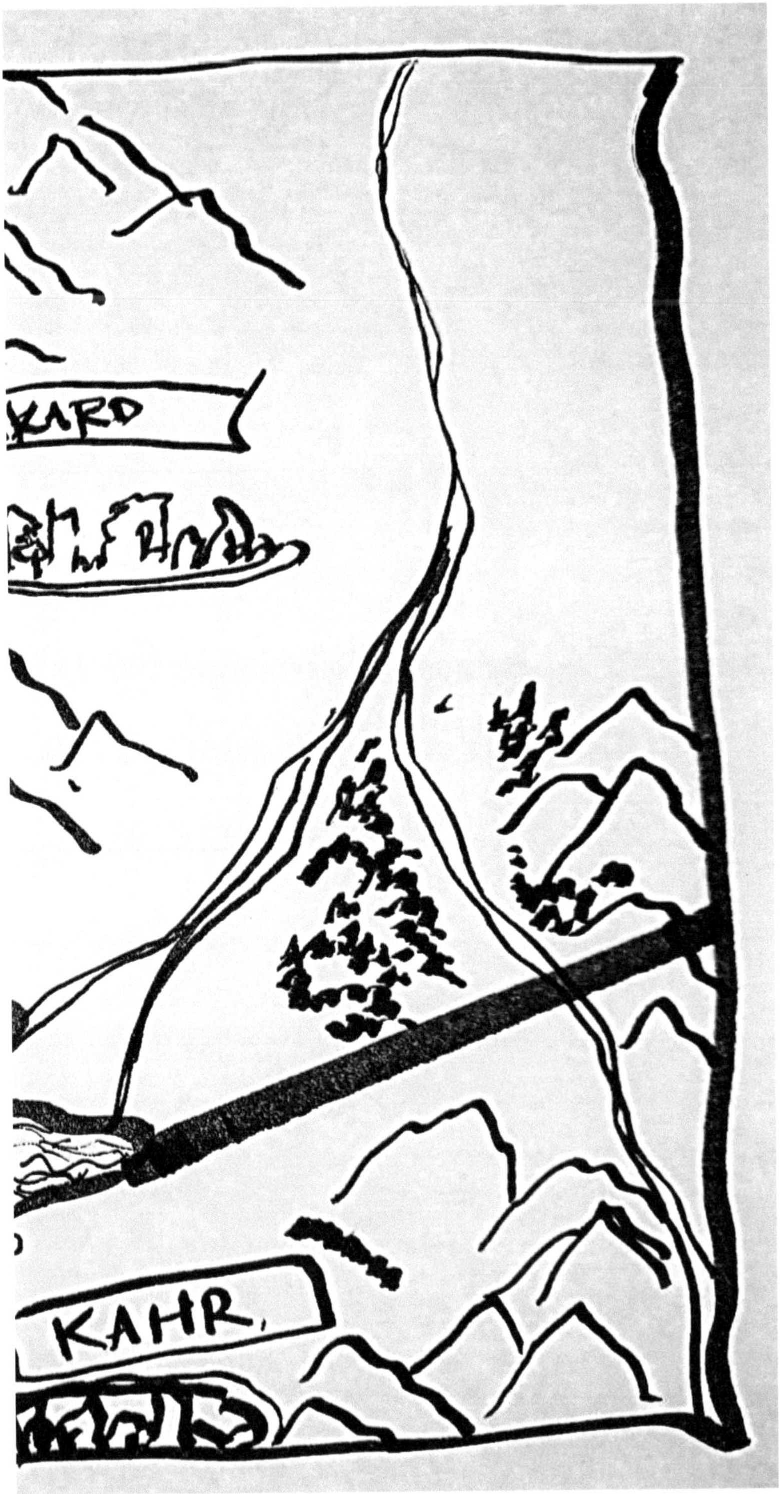
KARD
KAHR.

# Character Profiles

## Claudianne

**Birthdate:** Nivis's End, 127 Imperial Year

**Faction:** Mage-Born & Knight's Faction

**Rankings:** Archduke's Daughter, Princess, Sultana

**Stats Chart:**

| | | | | | | | | |
|---|---|---|---|---|---|---|---|---|
| Mage Mana | | | | | | | | |
| Knight's Aura | | | | | | | | |
| Adaptability | | | | | | | | |
| Battle Skill | | | | | | | | |
| Magic Ability | | | | | | | | |
| Intellect | | | | | | | | |

# Character Art

# Realistic Art Character Inspiration

# Character Profiles

## Johannes

**Birthdate:** Solaris's Gifts, 125 Imperial Year

**Faction:** Knight's Faction & Mage-Born

**Rankings:** Prince, Marquess's son, Sultan

**Stats Chart:**

| | | | | | | | | | | |
|---|---|---|---|---|---|---|---|---|---|---|
| Mage Mana | ■ | ■ | ■ | ■ | ■ | | | | | |
| Knight's Aura | ■ | ■ | ■ | ■ | ■ | ■ | ■ | | | |
| Adaptability | ■ | ■ | ■ | ■ | ■ | ■ | ■ | ■ | ■ | ■ |
| Battle Skill | ■ | ■ | ■ | ■ | ■ | ■ | ■ | ■ | ■ | |
| Magic Ability | ■ | ■ | ■ | ■ | | | ■ | ■ | ■ | ■ |
| Intellect | ■ | ■ | ■ | ■ | ■ | ■ | ■ | ■ | ■ | ■ |

## Character Art

## Realistic Art Character Inspiration

# Story Timeline

## 125 Imperial Year

**Solaris's Gifts –** Klaus Jakard is born, saved from the coup and brought up by Qassim Malik, named as "Klaus Malik" and hidden away.

## 127 Imperial Year

**Nivis's End –** Claudianne Jakard is born

## 139 Imperial Year

**Solaris's End –** Klaus saves Claudianne, is brought to the palace to become her personal guard

## 140 Imperial Year

**Seed's Sewn –** Claudianne forced to marry Kasha Fazar

## 142 Imperial Year

**Blizzard's Reign –** Claudianne miscarries, her mother dies

**Seed's Sewn –** Klaus and Claudianne copulate, Klaus leaves to the United Kingdom to seek help from his cousin, Ciel Twilight

**Veras's Height –** Klaus returns to Jakard kingdom, overthrows Kasha, is named Sultan, takes Claudianne as his Sultana

## 143 Imperial Year

**Nivis's End –** Kaleem Jakard is born

## 146 Imperial Year

Cavelle Jakard is born

## 149 Imperial Year

Kaia Jakard is born

## 150 Imperial Year

Kaia Jakard passes away

## 152 Imperial Year

Kadi Jakard is born

## 159 Imperial Year

**Seed's Sewn –** Kaleem Jakard marries Asra Ali

## 160 Imperial Year

Cavelle Jakard is adopted in United Empire, named Cavelle Jakard "Luther," marries Marielle Twilight

## 167 Imperial Year

Kadi Jakard marries Amin Ali

**MOVING TO THE ROYAL'S SAGA BOOK 7**

**THE DECOY DUCHESS**

**The Decoy Duchess is on a different Calendar System, for the United Empire – Imperial Lunar Year**

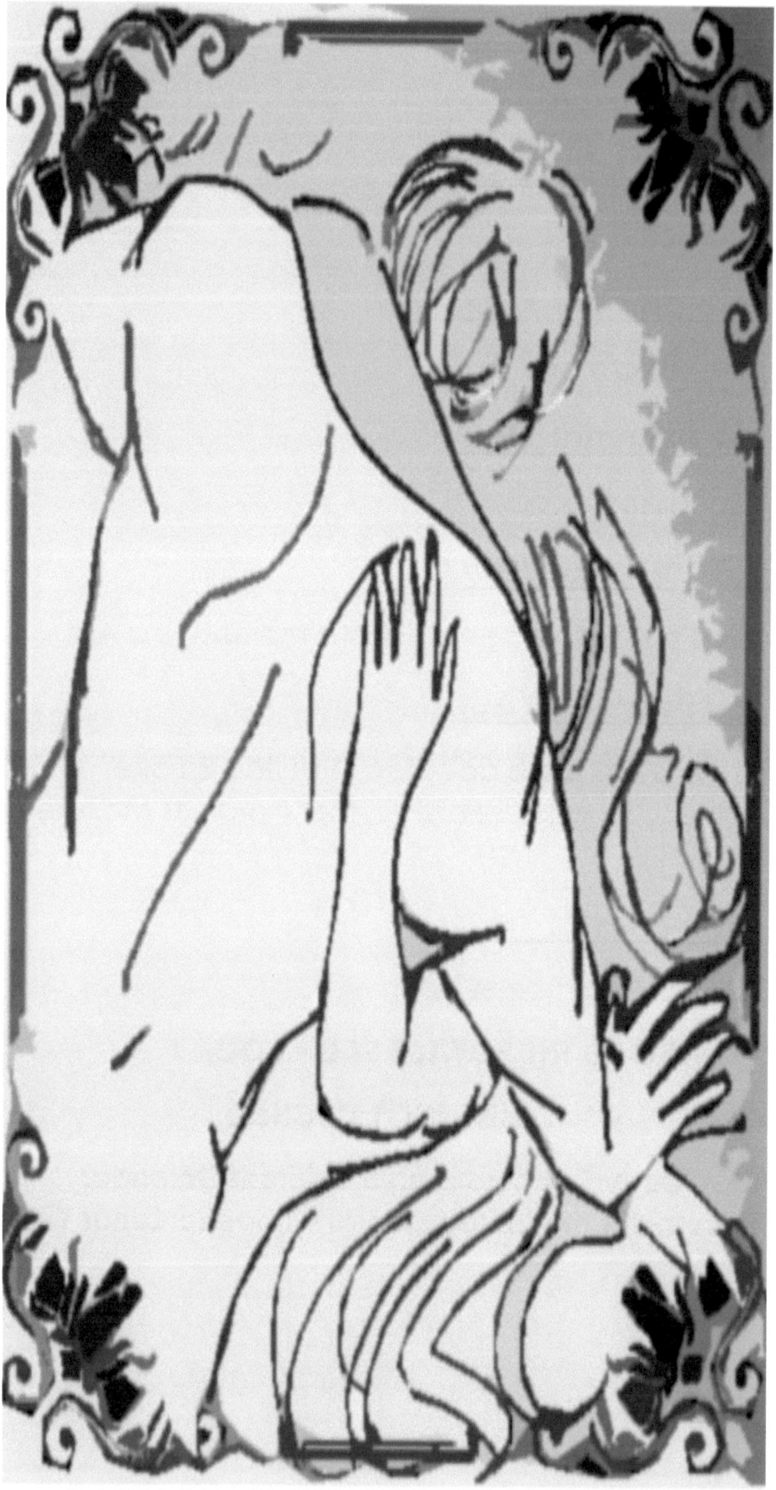

# The Decoy Duchess

# The Decoy Duchess Muse Playlist
### (Alphabetical Order)

**Book 7 Theme: Taylor Swift - Wonderland**

## Muse Playlist (Alphabetical Order)

1. 30 Seconds to Mars – Closer to the Edge
2. Brabo Gator – By Myself
3. Breaking Benjamin – Breakdown
4. CELINE theme: Peaceful Piano – Serenity
5. Clare Cunningham – CLOVERS
6. Clean Bandit ft Sean Paul – Rockabye
7. Citizen Soldier – I'm not Okay
8. Citizen Soldier – Make Hate to Me
9. Ellie Goulding – Hollow Crown
10. ERICH theme: Piano Dreamers – Snake Eyes (instrumental)
11. Eurythmics – Sweet Dreams (slowed & reverb)
12. Evanescence – Everybody's fool
13. Evanescence – Exodus
14. Fionn – 4 Leaf Clovers
15. Forest Blakk – I saw Love
16. GABRIELLE theme: Alexandre Pachabezian – River Flows in You
17. Il Volo – This time
18. Kelly Clarkson – Behind these Hazel eyes
19. Lil Nas X – Montero (Call me by your name)

20. Lindsey Stirling – Take Flight
21. Linkin Park – In the End
22. Metallica – My friend of Misery
23. Metallica – The Struggle Within
24. My Sun and Stars – You Stole my Heart
25. Neoni – Darkside
26. New West – Those Eyes
27. OsMan – Look at the Sky
28. Ruelle – I Get to Love You
29. Taylor Swift – Blank Space
30. Tiesto & Ava Max – The Motto (Slowed & Reverb)
31. VANDER theme: Ilya Beshievli – Compassion
32. Witchz – Wicked Game

# Family Tree

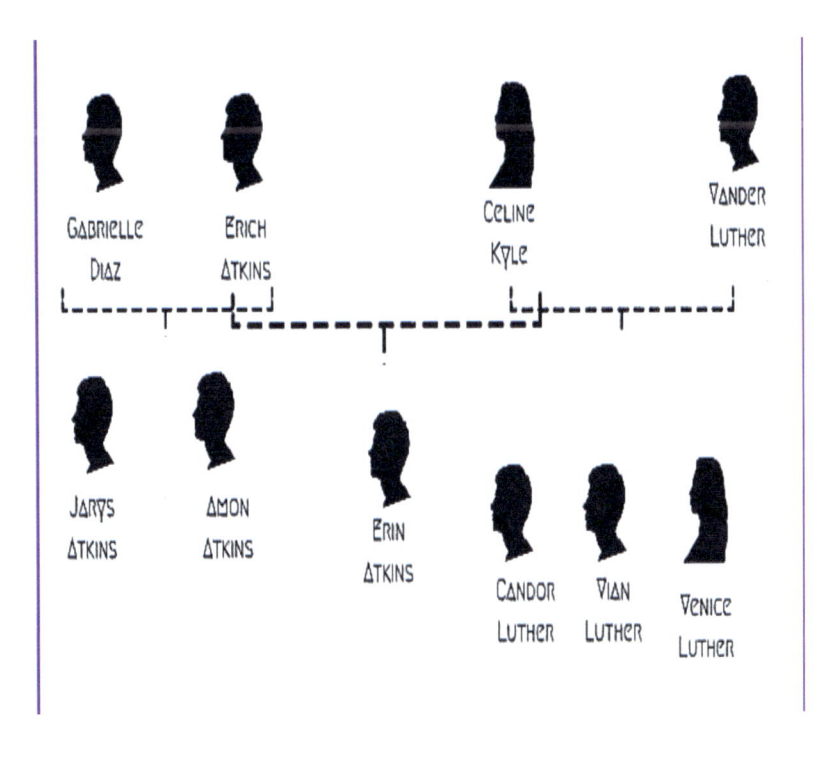

| Gabrielle Diaz | Erich Atkins | Celine Kyle | Vander Luther |

| Jarys Atkins | Amon Atkins | Erin Atkins | Candor Luther | Vian Luther | Venice Luther |

# Character Profiles
## Celine

**Birthdate:** Moon's Dance, 1080 Imperial Lunar Year

**Faction:** Mage-Born

**Rankings:** Baron's Daughter, Baroness, Duchess, Archduchess

**Stats Chart:**

|  | | | | | | | | |
|---|---|---|---|---|---|---|---|---|
| Mage Mana | ■ | ■ | ■ | ■ | ■ | ■ | ■ | |
| Knight's Aura | | | | | | | | |
| Adaptability | ■ | ■ | ■ | ■ | ■ | ■ | | |
| Battle Skill | | | | | | | | |
| Magic Ability | ■ | ■ | ■ | ■ | | | | |
| Intellect | ■ | ■ | ■ | ■ | ■ | ■ | ■ | |

# Character Art

# Realistic Art Character Inspiration

# Character Profiles

## Erich

**Birthdate:** Rain's Fall, 1079 Imperial Lunar Year

**Faction:** Knight Faction & Mage-Born

**Rankings:** Duke's son, Duke

**Stats Chart**

|  |  |
|---|---|
| Mage Mana | ▰▰▰▰▱▱▱▱▱▱ |
| Knight's Aura | ▰▰▰▱▱▱▱▱▱▱ |
| Adaptability | ▰▰▰▰▱▱▱▱▱▱ |
| Battle Skill | ▰▰▰▰▱▱▱▱▱▱ |
| Magic Ability | ▰▱▱▱▱▱▱▱▱▱ |
| Intellect | ▰▰▰▰▰▰▰▰▰▰ |

# Character Art

# Character Profiles

## Gabrielle

**Birthdate:** Veras's End, 1080 Imperial Lunar Year

**Faction:** Knight's Faction & Mage Born

**Rankings:** 3rd son of a Marquess, "Dutcher."

**Stats Chart**

|  | | | | | | | | | | |
|---|---|---|---|---|---|---|---|---|---|---|
| Mage Mana | ■ | ■ | | | | | | | | |
| Knight's Aura | ■ | | | | | | | | | |
| Adaptability | ■ | ■ | ■ | ■ | ■ | ■ | ■ | ■ | ■ | |
| Battle Skill | | | | | | | | | | |
| Magic Ability | ■ | ■ | | | | | | | | |
| Intellect | ■ | ■ | ■ | ■ | ■ | ■ | ■ | ■ | ■ | ■ |

# Character Art

## Realistic Art Character Inspiration

# Character Profiles
## Vander

**Birthdate:** Seed's Sewn, 1076 Imperial Lunar Year

**Faction:** Knight's Faction

**Rankings:** Prince, Archduke

**Stats Chart**

|  |  |
|---|---|
| Mage Mana | ■□□□□□□□□□ |
| Knight's Aura | ■■■■■■■■□□ |
| Adaptability | ■■■■■■■■□□ |
| Battle Skill | ■■■■■■□□□□ |
| Magic Ability | ■□□□□□□□□□ |
| Intellect | ■■■■■■■■■□ |

# Character Art

# Realistic Art Character Inspiration

# Story Timeline

## 1076 Imperial Lunar Year

**Seed's Sewn –** Vander Luther is born

## 1079 Imperial Lunar Year

**Rain's Fall –** Erich Atkins is born

## 1080 Imperial Lunar Year

**Veras's End –** Gabrielle Diaz is born

**Moon's Dance –** Kassondra "Celine" Kyle is born

## 1086 Imperial Lunar Year

**Solaris's End –** Baron Kyle passes away, leaving Celine's mother in debt and vulnerable.

## 1094 Imperial Lunar Year

**Solaris's End –** Celine's mother passes away

**Moon's Dance –** Celine rescued from the streets, taken into the Atkins duchy and signs a contract to marry Erich Atkins upon her 16th birthday

## 1096 Imperial Lunar Year

**Moon's Dance –** Erich and Celine marry

## 1098 Imperial Lunar Year

**Moon's Dance –** Erin Atkins is born, Duke Atkins is arrested, Erich and Celine divorce

## 1099 Imperial Lunar Year

**Nivis's End** – Vander Luther marries Celine

## 1101 Imperial Lunar Year

**Blizzard's Reign** – Vian and Candor Luther are born

## 1104 Imperial Lunar Year

**Folias's Blessing** – Venice Luther is born

**MOVING TO THE ROYAL'S SAGA BOOK 8**

**THE EMPATHETIC BROTHER**

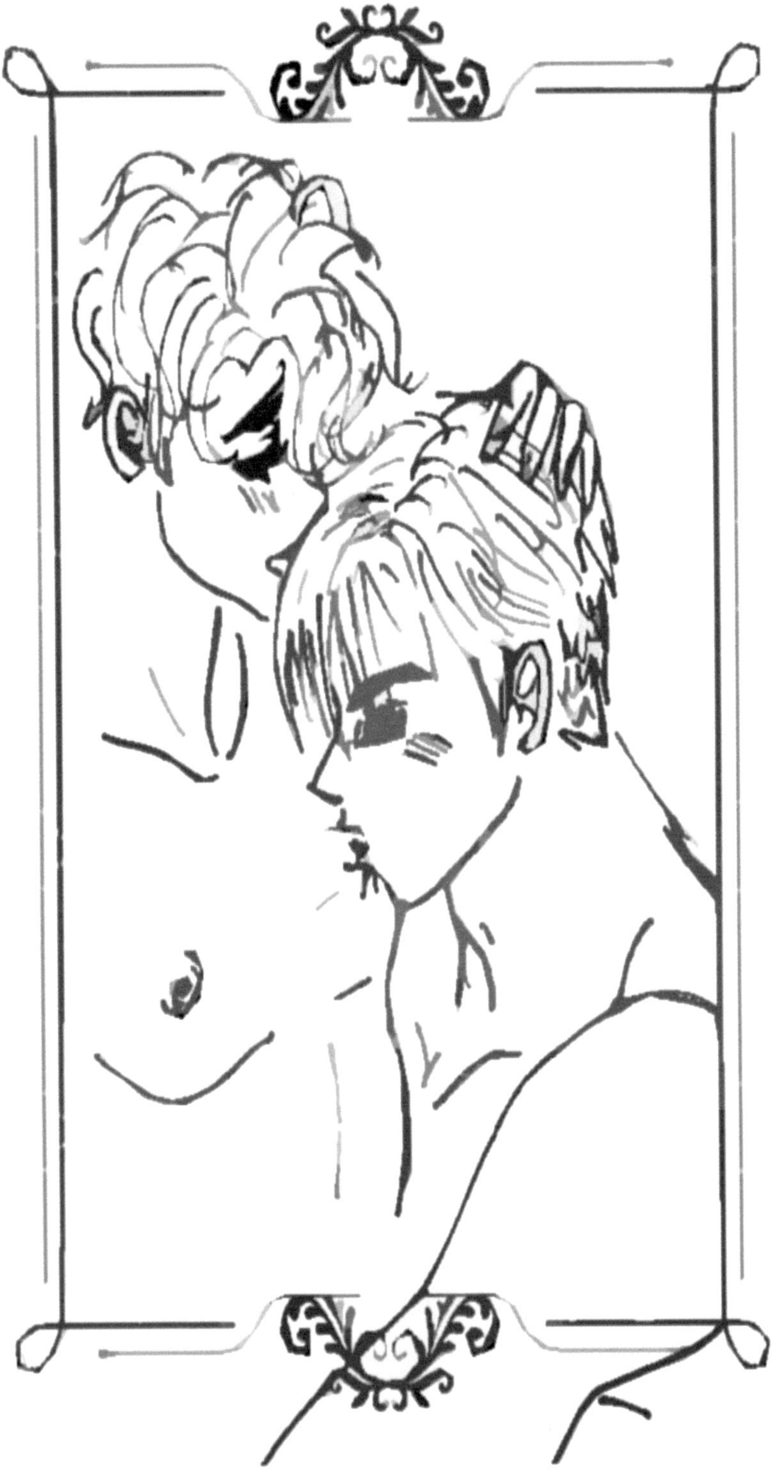

# The Empathetic Brother

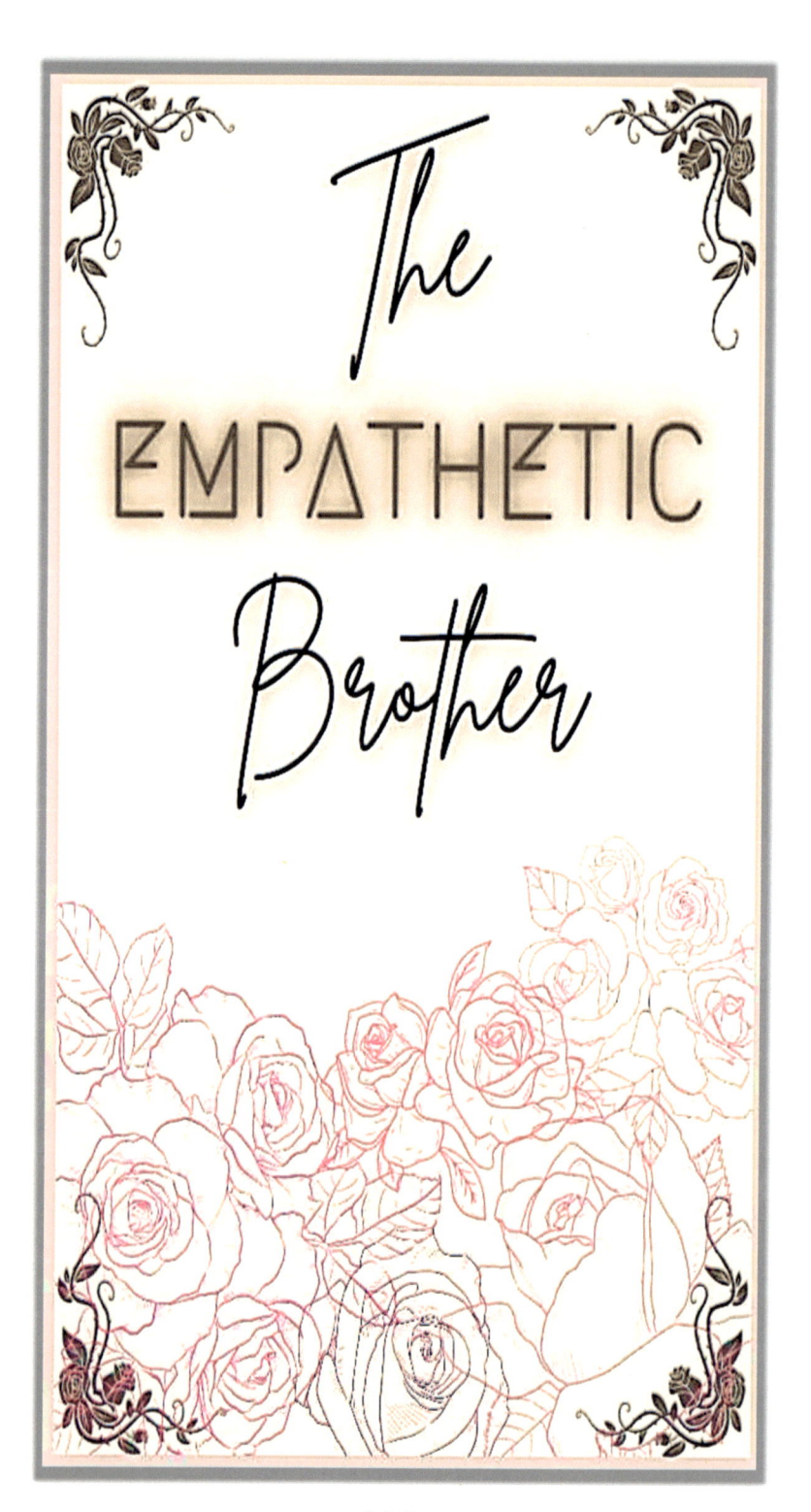

# The Empathetic Brother Muse Playlist

*(Alphabetical Order)*

**Book 8 Theme: Bring Me the Horizon - DArkSide**

## Muse Playlist (Alphabetical Order)

1. 30 Seconds to Mars – From Yesterday
2. American Authors – Luck
3. Anastacia – Take This Chance
4. Billy Squire – Emotions in Motion
5. Billy Squire – Rock me tonight
6. Bon Jovi – Bed of Roses
7. Camila Cabello – Havana
8. Breaking Benjamin – Give me a Sign
9. Breaking Benjamin – The Diary of Janes
10. Bullet for My Valentine – Tears Don't Fall
11. Citizen Soldier – Death of Me
12. Citizen Soldier – Unbreakable
13. Clean Bandit – Rather Be
14. Cody Johnson – 'til You Can't
15. Elise Azkoul – La Vie En Rose
16. Evanescence – Cloud 9
17. Evanescence – Lacrymosa
18. Imminence – Heaven in Hiding
19. In this Moment – Forever
20. Linkin Park – No More Sorrow
21. Motionless In White: Another Life (disguise)

22. KATHRYN THEME: 2CELLOS – We found Love
23. KENNETH THEME: Max-Music – Tension
24. KILLIAN THEME: 2CELLOS – Use Somebody
25. Little mix – Change your Life
26. Paloma Faith – Only Love Can Hurt Like This
27. Seether – Fine Again
28. The Chainsmokers – Roses
29. Three Days Grace – Break
30. Tool – Schism
31. Queen Naija – Butterflies
**32.** Witchz – Seasons

# Family Tree

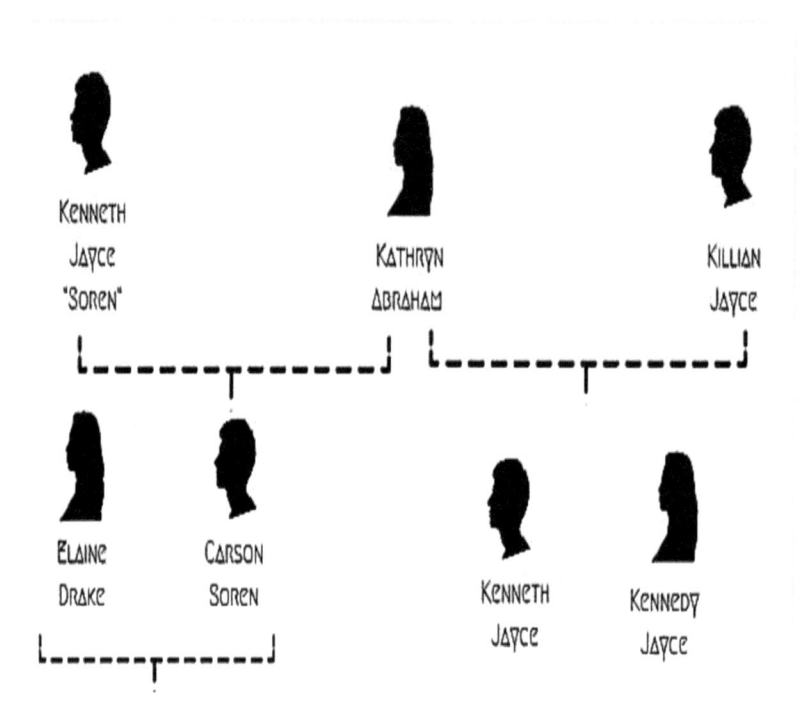

Kenneth Jayce "Soren"  —  Kathryn Abraham  —  Killian Jayce

Elaine Drake — Carson Soren

Kenneth Jayce

Kennedy Jayce

# Character Profiles

## Kathryn

**Birthdate:** Moon's Dance, 1300 Imperial Lunar Year

**Faction:** Mage-Born

**Rankings:** Marquess's illegitimate Daughter, Marchioness, Duchess

**Stats Chart:**

|  | | | | | | | | | | |
|---|---|---|---|---|---|---|---|---|---|---|
| Mage Mana | █ | █ | █ | | | | | | | |
| Knight's Aura | | | | | | | | | | |
| Adaptability | █ | █ | █ | █ | | | | | | |
| Battle Skill | | | | | | | | | | |
| Magic Ability | █ | | | | | | | | | |
| Intellect | █ | █ | █ | █ | █ | █ | █ | █ | | |

# Character Art

**Realistic Art Character Inspiration**

# Character Profiles

## Killian

**Birthdate:** Nivis's End, 1297 Imperial Lunar Year

**Faction:** Knight Faction

**Rankings:** Duke's son, Duke

**Stats Chart**

|  |  |
|---|---|
| Mage Mana | █ |
| Knight's Aura | █████ |
| Adaptability | ██████▒▒█ |
| Battle Skill | ████ |
| Magic Ability | |
| Intellect | █████████ |

## Character Art

**Realistic Art Character Inspiration**

# Character Profiles

## Kenneth

**Birthdate:** Solaris's Reign, 1298 Imperial Lunar Year

**Faction:** Knight's Faction

**Rankings:** 2nd son of a Duke, heir to his Marquess grandfather, Marquess

### Stats Chart

| Stat | 1 | 2 | 3 | 4 | 5 | 6 | 7 | 8 | 9 |
|---|---|---|---|---|---|---|---|---|---|
| Mage Mana | | | | | | | | | |
| Knight's Aura | ■ | ■ | ■ | ■ | ■ | | | | |
| Adaptability | ■ | ■ | ■ | ■ | ■ | ■ | ■ | ■ | |
| Battle Skill | ■ | ■ | | | | | | | |
| Magic Ability | | | | | | | | | |
| Intellect | ■ | ■ | ■ | ■ | ■ | ■ | ■ | | |

# Character Art

## Realistic Art Character Inspiration

# Story Timeline

## 1297 Imperial Lunar Year

**Nivis's End** – Killian Jayce is born

## 1298 Imperial Lunar Year

**Solaris's Reign** – Kenneth Jayce Soren is born

## 1300 Imperial Lunar Year

**Moon's Dace** – Kathryn Abraham is born

## 1314 Imperial Lunar Year

**Moon's Dance** – Kenneth and Kathryn married, named Marquess and Marchioness

## 1315 Imperial Lunar Year

**Solaris's Reign** – Carson Soren is born

## 1316 Imperial Lunar Year

**Veras's Height** – Kenneth Soren is murdered, Soren Marquessate burned down, Kathryn and Carson go to the Abraham Marquessate

**Folias's Blessing** – Killian Jayce rescues Kathryn from Abraham Marquessate, brings her and Carson to the Jayce duchy to live with him

## 1317 Imperial Lunar Year

**Veras's End** – Killian confesses his feelings to Kathryn, and they begin courting officially

**Folias's Blessing** – Killian discovers Kenneth's murderers

**Year's Fall –** Killian and Kathryn marry

## 1318 Imperial Lunar Year

**Solaris's Reign –** Marquess and Marchioness Abraham arrested for Kenneth Soren's murder

## 1319 Imperial Lunar Year

**Seed's Sewn –** Kenneth Jayce is born

## 1320 Imperial Lunar Year

**Solaris's Gifts –** Kennedy Jayce is born

## 1335 Imperial Lunar Year

**Solaris's End –** Carson Soren marries Elaine Drake

**MOVING TO THE ROYAL'S SAGA BOOK 9**

**THE ANONYMOUS WRITER**

# The ANONYMOUS Writer

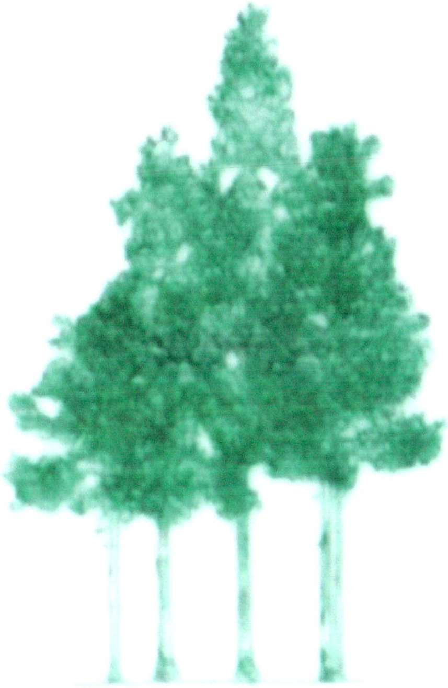

# The Anonymous Writer Muse Playlist

*(Alphabetical Order)*

**Book 9 Theme: Il Volo – Hasta El Final**

## Muse Playlist (Alphabetical Order)

1. 30 Seconds to Mars – Closer to the Edge
2. Avicii – Wake me Up
3. Billy Squire – Don't say you love me
4. Billy Squire – Don't let me go
5. Breaking Benjamin – Breakdown
6. Breaking Benjamin – Forget it
7. Breaking Benjamin – Had enough
8. CADENCE Theme – Piano Lounge Club – Snow is Falling
9. CONSTANCE Theme – 2Cellos – Vivaldi Storm
10. Citizen Soldier – Make hate to me
11. Citizen Soldier – Thank you for hating me
12. Disturbed – The Night
13. Disturbed – Warrior
14. Ellie Goulding – Starry Eyed
15. Evanescence – Whisper
16. Imagine Dragons - Thunder
17. In this Moment – Standing Alone
18. Korn – Liar
19. Nightwish – End of all hope
20. Nightwish – Gethsemane

21. Sam Tinnesz – Play with Fire
22. Skylar Grey – Coming Home
23. Staind – For You
24. Sparks to the Rescue – Pine Tree State
25. Tears for Fears – Shout
26. Three Days Grace – Time of Dying
27. Twenty-One Pilots – Heathens
28. Two Steps from Hell – Enigmatic Soul
29. Two Steps from Hell - Winterspell
30. WITCHZ – The Witch
31. Within Temptation – Hills of mist
32. Within Temptation – Our Solemn Hour

# Family Tree

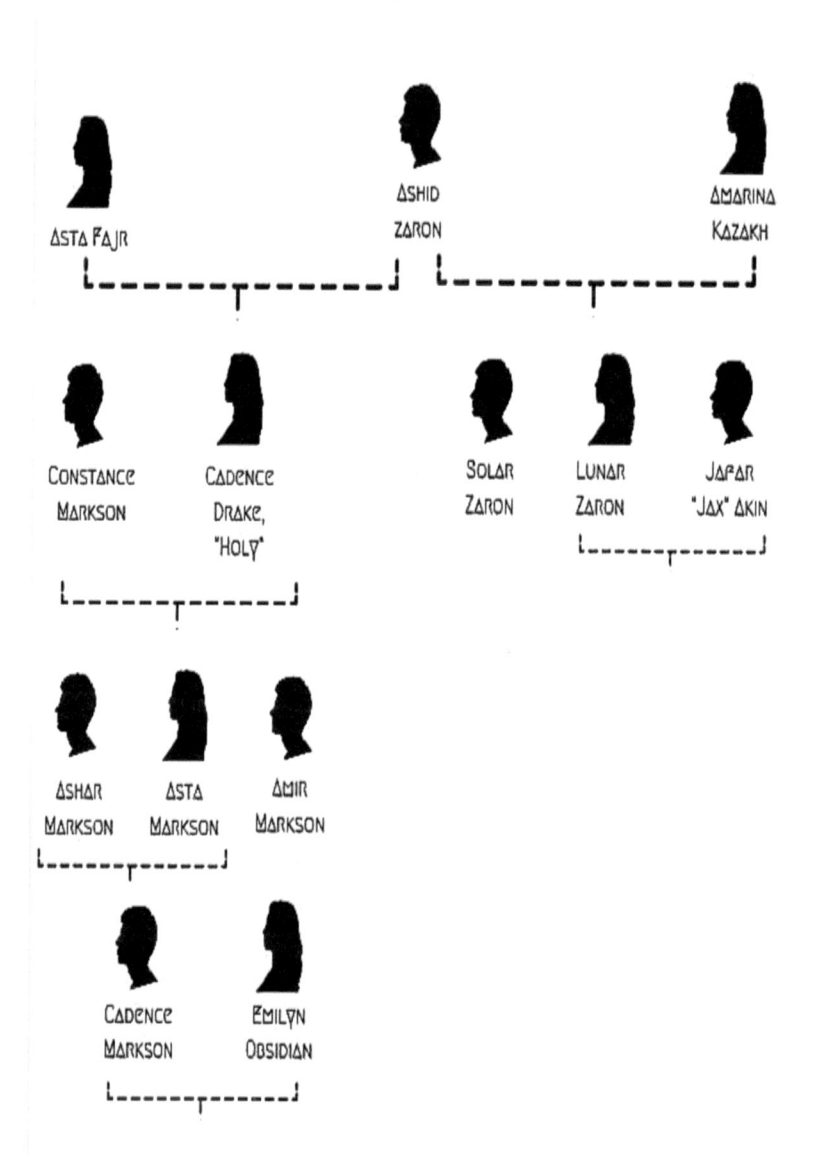

- **Asta Fajr** — **Ashid Zaron** — **Amarina Kazakh**
  - Constance Markson — Cadence Drake, "Holy"
    - Ashar Markson — Asta Markson — Amir Markson
      - Cadence Markson — Emilyn Obsidian
  - Solar Zaron
  - Lunar Zaron — Jafar "Jax" Akin

# Character Profiles

### Cadence Drake

**Birthdate:** Solaris's Reign, 1502 Imperial Lunar Year

**Faction:** Mage-Born

**Rankings:** Archduke's daughter

**Stats Chart:**

|  | | | | | | | | | |
|---|---|---|---|---|---|---|---|---|---|
| Mage Mana | ■ | ■ | ■ | ■ | ■ | ■ | ■ | | |
| Knight's Aura | | | | | | | | | |
| Adaptability | ■ | ■ | ■ | ■ | ■ | ■ | | | |
| Battle Skill | | | | | | | | | |
| Magic Ability | ■ | ■ | ■ | ■ | ■ | ■ | ■ | | |
| Intellect | ■ | ■ | ■ | ■ | ■ | ■ | ■ | ■ | ■ |

# Character Art

# Realistic Art Character Inspiration

# Character Profiles

## Constance

**Birthdate:** Seed's Sewn, 1499 Imperial Lunar Year

**Faction:** Knight Faction

**Rankings:** Marquess's 3rd son

### Stats Chart

|  |  |
|---|---|
| Mage Mana | 1 |
| Knight's Aura | 8 |
| Adaptability | 7 |
| Battle Skill | 6 |
| Magic Ability | 2 |
| Intellect | 3 |

# Character Art

# Realistic Art Character Inspiration

# Story Timeline

## 1499 Imperial Lunar Year

**Seed's Sewn –** Constance Markson born

## 1502 Imperial Lunar Year

**Solaris's Reign –** Cadence Drake is born

## 1516 Imperial Lunar Year

**Rain's Fall –** Constance becomes Cadence's anonymous pen-pal

## 1519 Imperial Lunar Year

**Solaris's Gifts –** Cadence's secret tryst is discovered, she uncovers her pen-pal's true identity, runs from forced marriage to the Jakard Kingdom

**Solaris's End –** Lands in Jakard kingdom, discovers her father's true identity, meets her father Ashid. She is renamed "Holy," and marries Constance

## 1520 Imperial Lunar Year

**Veras's End –** Ashar Markson is born

## 1522 Imperial Lunar Year

**Solaris's Gifts –** Asta Markson is born

## 1534 Imperial Lunar Year

Amir Markson is born

## 1542 Imperial Lunar Year

**Solaris's End –** Ashar and Asta marry

# 1546 Imperial Lunar Year

**Moon's Dance –** Cadence Markson is born

**MOVING INTO THE ROYAL'S SAGA BOOK 10: THE LUXURIOUS SLAVE**

# Requested Bonus Chapter:

This extra content chapter was requested by multiple fans, and so here it is! A P.O.V. chapter from hot, sleek, Dark-Magic Dark-Sorcerer daddy himself;

## Ashid Zaron

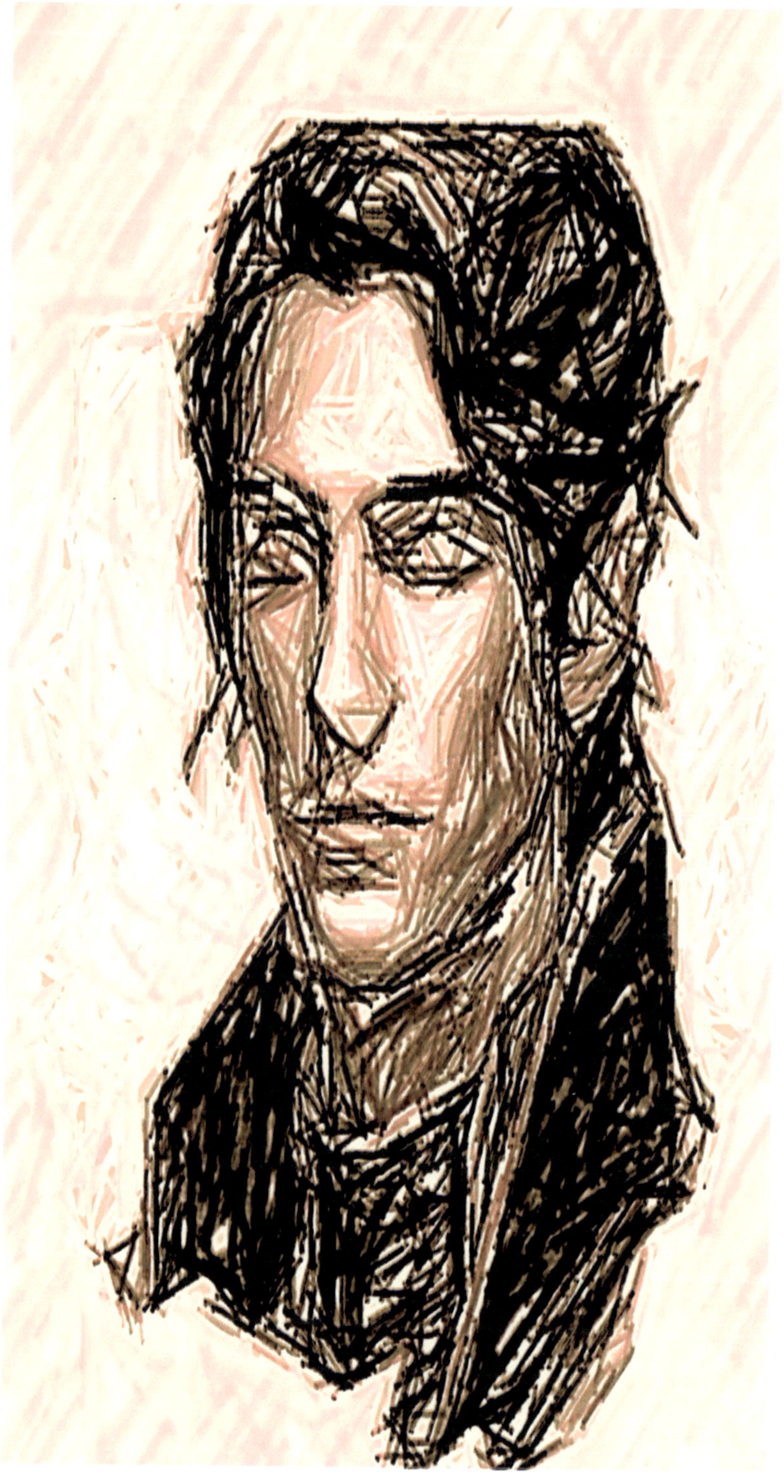

# *Ashid Zaron...*

## *Solaris's End, 1499 Imperial Lunar Year*

I sat at the edge of the forest, breathing heavily as my aide left my side, rushing off to get my guards.

I had been spotted by some of the coup-plotter bastard's men, and had been attacked before I could even seek help for my cause in this country I had been forced to run to.

My father, the Archduke Zaron in the country of Kahr, had been overthrown by my uncle.

I had been targeted as well, but I had run, making my way to local kingdoms around to try to seek help in promise for riches.

This time, however, I had been caught off-guard, being in this city for a peace treaty meeting. It was my perfect chance to strike a deal for help.

The first time that met her...would turn out to be rather unconventional. I never expected to find the love of my life in such a place, in such a vulnerable state.

She found me among the edge of the forest, injured from an arrow to the side.

"O-Oh, heavens!" She cried, rushing over to me.

"Stay calm," I told her. "Just be quiet, and don't draw attention to me..." I groaned.

"I-I know how to help," she told me...and so, she had quickly helped me, terrified of the repercussions of anyone finding a mage injured in Knight-ruled lands. The alliance would be broken, for sure.

"We have to take care that nobody finds you here," she said. "It would ruin the negotiations for peace!"

She had broken off the end of the arrow already, and then she gave me a little warning and forced it the rest of the way through, before she had cauterized the wound.

"I...think that we can move for now," she told me, helping me up to my feet. "My chambers are not far from here. Do you think you can walk with me a hundred feet?"

I nodded, and leaned on her as she walked me to her bedchambers and her gardens.

She surprised me further when she got out a first-aid kit, and pulled me out to the gardens. She set to work, and treated me in her own private guest room—in the garden's aviary, where only *she* was allowed to attend to.

I loved her already.

She was so...smart and quick-witted, but so naïve, as well.

She knew how to treat my wounds, as if she had training, but she had taken a random strange man—an injured man, yes, but still—to her private bedchambers in a foreign land and was working over his partially naked body without even asking questions? Or, even a single question...?

What was wrong with this girl?

She was stunning, though. She had pale skin, for one of our people, and sooty-black hair. Her eyes were mesmerizing, a beautiful, moody, almost maroon-mixed lavender. They drew me in, making me want to sink into them...

Sink into her...

"What is your name?" I asked her.

"What is yours?" She countered, and I chuckled.

"Ashid," I told her. "You?"

She paused, but she finally smiled and sighed, raising an eyebrow at me.

"Asta."

I smirked at her, and began to slowly pull my pointer finger up and down her bare arm, before tingling the tinkling bangle-bracelets on her wrist.

"Are you...attached?" I asked, giving her the smoldering gaze that I knew, from experience, made women weak at the knees. "I don't see a wedding band or engagement ring."

She giggled, batting her lashes at me. "I am not married. I am not engaged."

"I see. What brings you to this place?" I asked her. "You mentioned the peace treaty. Are you here as part of a peace delegation?"

"Yes," she nodded. "I am part of the delegation from Jakard. I am the Archduke's daughter. The sultan is my uncle."

"I see," I said, stricken by our status similarity. "I am also the child of an Archduke, and nephew to the sultan."

"Oh," she gaped at me. "I..." she gawked at her hands on my bare torso, and her face flushed. "I-I'm so sorry, I—"

I waved it off. "You saved my life. I would have been in trouble if you hadn't found me when you had...and I never would have met the love of my life."

She faltered, eyes wide and gasping at me. "Your grace—"

"'Ashid,' please, and...as I just learned, recently, life is short. You never know what is going to happen, and when your life may just be cut short."

"...I see your point," she said, blushing at me and looking at my torso again. "You...are truly beautiful," she breathed.

I chuckled. "You took the words out of my mouth. You are stunning."

She blushed again, and began to prattle on about random things—from flowers and plants, to Mages and Knights, to anything and everything in between—all without hardly taking a breath.

I watched her with amused fascination, letting her talk wildly and animatedly without a pause.

It wasn't until the sun was setting that she seemed to notice, as she started struggling to see me in the growing dimness of the greenhouse aviary.

"W-what...what happened?" She asked, stunned.

"You were enjoying talking to me," I said, watching her with warmth.

She blushed, from her collar bone to her forehead and her ears.

"Y-you let me just r-ramble on and on..."

"I was enjoying your voice," I told her.

She let out a pent-up breath, staring at me in stunned silence. "You...you are amazing."

"I think I am dull in comparison," I told her. "You shine brightly."

"Speaking of shining," she said, rushing to move to the door. "I need to fetch a light—"

I put mana into my finger, shooting up a mana-ball of light into the center of the room, and she gasped and gawked at me.

"What—"

"I am a sorcerer," I informed her. "This is a parlor trick compared to my true power."

"...You are a sorcerer?"

I cringed, ready for her to be intimidated and run.

Anyone could tell, from my pure-black hair and dark, heavy golden-orange eyes, that I was a Dark Sorcerer.

What if she was afraid of me, now?

"I've never met one before, but that is amazing!" She smiled at me. "I am Mage-Born, but I never presented any power."

She seemed ashamed of this, but if her father was the Archduke in Jakard...then that would check out and make sense.

I smiled at her, and began telling her about magic that she could practice, even with little to no mana. Stones that could help her.

It was my turn to ramble.

By the end of the night, she got me a blanket to sleep on the lounge-chair on, and I woke up to a cup of warm coffee and a plate of delicious food the following morning...as well as a beautiful smile.

The days passed quickly, and on the fourth day, I managed to make my way back to the room that I had rented with my aide—and was bombarded by an emotional, worried friend, who hugged me and questioned me nearly to death.

A few more days passed, and I saw her out and about with her delegation.

As the peace coalition started to wrap up their business and I managed to find a sponsor who would help me and win my place back...

I had to think of something, a way to have her.

I had achieved everything else that I wanted to get done here, but there was no way that I could just leave her behind here and be okay with never seeing her again.

I had to have her, as my own.

She was, truly, the love of my life. I had never felt this way about anyone else, before.

In front of everyone, on the last day of the banquet—the large, ending party—I had finally found her; spotted her from my place where I was performing fire magics for the young sultan of that kingdom, as he clapped and laughed and enjoyed the show...and I made a decision.

I left the stage, mid-performance, to join her at her place.

It had nearly started a national crisis, but when she had stood, as if by pure instinct and feeling, and she had danced and laughed with me, her parents—whom had joined the delegation to this nation for the last day of the banquet, specifically for this festival event—had begun concocting a plan to get her in an arranged marriage with someone else...and quickly.

They weren't quite quick enough, however.

That night, I would ask for her hand in marriage, and we would lay with one another intimately.

I would undress her slowly, and gently peel of her silk gown, before I untied her bindings and let them fall to the floor.

My mouth would find purchase on her breasts, sucking her pert nipples into my mouth and gently nibbling on them as my hand groped her tight ass in my grip.

My body would become bare, and I would roll my hips gently as I pressed my cock into her heat, gasping and feeling heaven surround me as I felt her barrier give way to me.

I would leave my marks all over her chest and shoulders as I moved within her, listening to her airy gasps and feeling her desperate clutching at me with her hands, digging her fingernails into my shoulder-blades and leaving wounds.

I felt myself giving her my very heart as her warm, tight pussy clenched over me, fluttering and spurring me on.

I lost myself, filling her up and forever marking her as mine with my cum and mana that I released inside of her with it...giving her literal essence from myself, and almost ensuring that she would become pregnant by doing so.

I knew that it was wrong, but I was a dark and possessive bastard, and I wanted her to be mine.

The small streak of blood on my cock from my having taken her innocence was all that I needed to know that she belonged to me, and I was her first. It filled me with a beastly instinct to devour her and keep her locked away inside of me forever.

## Moon's Dance, 1499 Imperial Lunar Year

She had been ready to accept my hand in marriage, no matter *who* liked it...until the order was issued from the sultan of Jakard.

The order was that she was to marry the Archduke Drake, from the United Empire, who had just happened to be there a couple of months later, this time for an alliance banquet in her *own* nation.

She had *tried* to refuse, but her father had demanded it, and she had even been apprehended trying to run away.

I heard about this from an inside-friend that I had placed in the archduke's palace as a hand-maiden—my best friend's sister, to be exact—and she was passing letters back and forth between us.

Asta tried to fight it, refusing and refusing...

We even managed to get together again, having secret rendezvous and making love under the stars, in the desert...

She finally agreed to marry the archduke, however, and tried to convince me to stay out of it for my safety...but when I had gone against her wishes and tried to demand to be allowed to marry her behind her back, I had been beaten and tortured for trying to stop the marriage.

That...hadn't been fun.

I had been tempted to tell her father that I had been having his daughter for a while, now, and that my seed and mana were slowly growing and cultivating and waiting for the right time to be planted into her womb...

I knew, however, that this would just compromise her and put her in jeopardy, so I had to hold my tongue.

Her father and the archduke she was engaged had been convinced that it was her final attempt to avoid the marriage, and boycott their will, by having me try to get in the way...so they decided to use me against her, instead.

Her father had told her that she *had* to marry this foreign archduke to save my life, or they'd kill me then and there.

The sultan, her uncle, had vowed that if she did not marry for this alliance, her entire family would be killed.

So, in the end, she was forced wed the archduke.

## Year's Fall, 1499 Imperial Lunar Year

"You *can't!*" She sobbed, holding my arm. "You know that you can't go against the sultan! They would kill us both!"

"But you are *mine!*" I shouted fiercely, tugging away from her, and pacing in a panic. My long, inky, blue-toned pure black hair whished around with my movement, almost like a cape. "Why did the man have to choose you? You are already mine!"

"...My father," She whispered. "He doesn't approve of us. You know that he was already looking to get us away from each other! He doesn't know who you truly are—"

"Then let me tell them!" I raged. I knew I already had, and that they had no reason to agree with me as long as I hid my true identity, but still...

"You'd be in danger!" She sobbed. "No, Ashid! Remember...your uncle is hunting you. You cannot give yourself up this way!"

"I am not a Dark Sorcerer so that I can fear what may happen to me, and allow what is mine to be taken! I became a Dark Sorcerer to take back what is mine!"

"Then take it back!" She cried. "Take me back...when the time is right, and you have an army of mages at your back to fight for your cause."

"But Asta," I said, taking her into my arms and burying my nose and thick lips along the lobe of her ear, all around her neck, along her collarbone. "You belong to *me*," I said, resting a gentle hand over her belly.

My seed had finally chosen to plant inside of her, done cultivating, and it was rotted deeply in her body.

"Your womb is enriched with my seed. I cannot allow you to be taken, my midnight sky and my twinkling dawn star."

Her eyes welled with tears. She had only recently discovered the pregnancy.

"It is what we must do, for now. My father has already received the order of the sultan, and the sultan has already promised to hand me over. If we do not follow this act of goodwill, the alliance could break forever, and no matter how much you may say that we don't need it, the truth is that...we wouldn't be where we are, as a newly formed empire, without their help. If I don't obey, then the sultan will have my family killed. Their alliance and supplies and trade with Jakard is what has helped my nation to grow. Your own nation has benefited from it." She pressed her lips to mine. "But I promise you...if you come for me, I will leave with you. So, I need that from you, my love. Promise me...promise me you'll come for us."

"I swear it."

"Good." She kissed me again. "Now...come and save me and our child when you have become the *true* archduke. Once the victory is won...once you seize your life back...come for us."

I nodded. "I vow it. For you...and for our daughter," I said, kneeling down to rain kisses all over her still-flat belly.

"Daughter?" She asked, smiling. "You continue to call the child a girl—"

"I told you," I chuckled. "I've seen the child in my dreams. The moment you told me you were carrying my child, that very night, I dreamt of a daughter. I believe it was a divine sign from the heavens. Surely, I will come for you, my ladies. My loves."

We heard voices approaching her chambers, and I lingeringly pressed mournful kisses to her lips, cheeks, hair—whatever I could reach on me to kiss—before I slipped silently out of her bedroom window at the last possible moment, and disappeared in a cyclone of black sand...

Before her maids stepped in, preparing me to be debuted before her new fiancé.

## Year's Fall, 1507 Imperial Lunar Year

It had taken me several years to come into my power as the archduke and overthrow my uncle, but my first move had been to come to the United Empire, and begin searching for my love.

Only, rather quickly...I had heard whispers of her death.

Death...?

That couldn't be...

Still, despite the desperate aching in my heart and the pain spearing my insides, I used my magic to locate my seed and essence.

It had led me to where I now stood—standing before the castle of Archduke Drake.

My child...was inside here.

I knocked on the door, and the butler opened the door and inquired about my identity, before they summoned the lady of the castle—whom was the typical person responsible for greeting guests.

The woman who stepped into the foyer and gaped at me was, most certainly, *not my Asta...*

"And you are?" She asked, crossing her arms.

I could tell, from her foul-smelling perfume and gaudy tastes, that she was poor originally. She was noble by birth; I was certain of it.

"I am Archduke Zaron, from the country of Kahr. I am here for Archduchess Asta and her child."

She gaped at me, face turning beet red and sputtering out unattractively. "She is gone, and so is that child!" She shrieked. "I am the mistress of this castle! How dare you come here and demand things from me!? Do not bother us again! Away with you! Away, damn you! Before I call authorities!"

She had me ushered out, and the doors slammed shut behind me.

...Had I been wrong?

I spiraled into despair, my heart shattering to pieces in my chest.

Had she abandoned me? Decided to hide away?

I knew that she had married Archduke Drake...there was no way that she was not here, but I couldn't track her, as she was no longer filled with my mana and my seed.

Tracking the child had led me here, but they had turned me away.

So...what was I to do?

I cringed, as the rain began to pour, and thunder cracked around me.

I knew that my mana was reacting to my anger and hurt.

The storm was a product of my rage and pain.

I would never be the same.

I had never even gotten to meet my child...and though I couldn't see the future, I had hoped that I would get to, and get to be her father, and raise her. Love her.

The daughter of my true love and myself.

I loved the children that I had, now, but it wasn't the same. They were conceived and born out of duty and necessity, but they weren't made in love.

One day, however, many years later...

I would meet a lovely young woman.

She would have my hair, and her mother's skin. She would have my eyes mixed with her mother's, and she would be shy and kind and sweet.

I would rename her, and she would marry her true love and live happily, as a family, with me and her husband and their children forevermore.

My life, though full of suffering and pain, would finally become bliss.

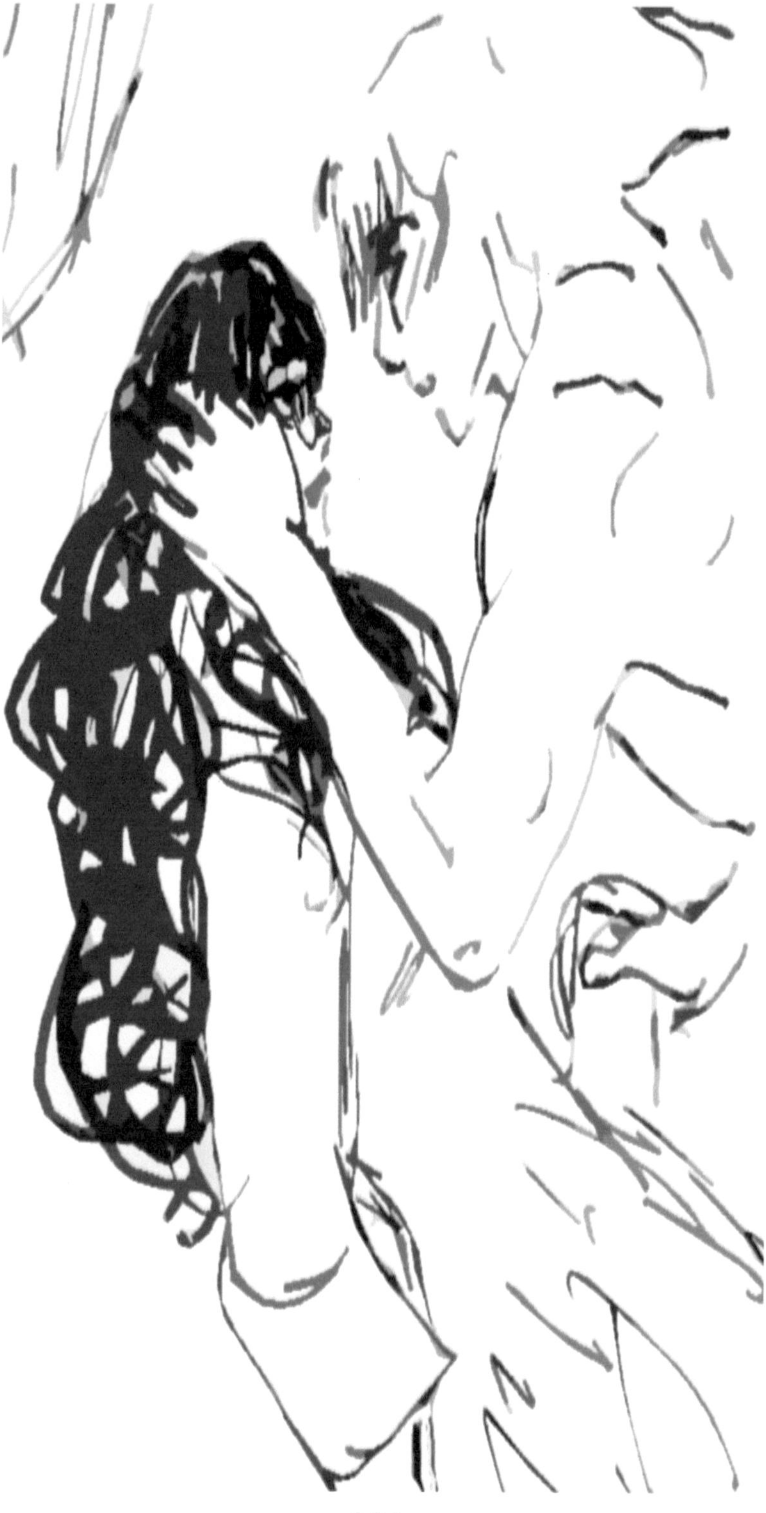

# The Luxurious Slave

# The Luxurious Slave Muse Playlist

*(Alphabetical Order)*

**Book 10 Theme: Lindsey Stirling – Masquerade**

## Muse Playlist (Alphabetical Order)

1. Adeline Hill – Moments to Memories
2. Andrea Vanzo – Soul Mate
3. Argy & Omnya – Aria
4. Avenged Sevenfold – So Far Away
5. Avicii – Wake me Up
6. Battled – Black Dahlias
7. Breaking Benjamin – Break
8. Camila Cabello – Shameless
9. CHROME THEME: Bones – Chrome
10. Citizen Soldier – Hope it Haunts You
11. CLANN – Caves
12. Danjerr – Monents
13. Deeprise, Eneli – Dahlia Girl
14. Demeter – Slow Down
15. Demeter – Uhu
16. Demeter & Ticia – Good Girl
17. Ellie Goulding – By the End of the Night
18. Evanescence – Snow White Queen
19. Evanescence – Your Star
20. Falling in Reverse – Watch the World Burn

21. Jessie J – Masterpiece
22. KYLIE THEME: HA&GO – Snow Storm
23. Lindsey Stirling – Snow Waltz
24. Mariah Carey – Obsessed
25. Matt Gorman – Little things
26. Nation Heaven – Morally Grey
27. Oh, Hush! – Happy Place
28. Oh The Larceny – Man on a Mission
29. OsMan – Look at the Sky
30. Our Last Night – Middle of the Night
31. Sara Bareilles – Brave
32. Skald – Seven Nation Army
33. Skyfall Beats – Night Vibe WITCHZ – Charmer

# Family Tree

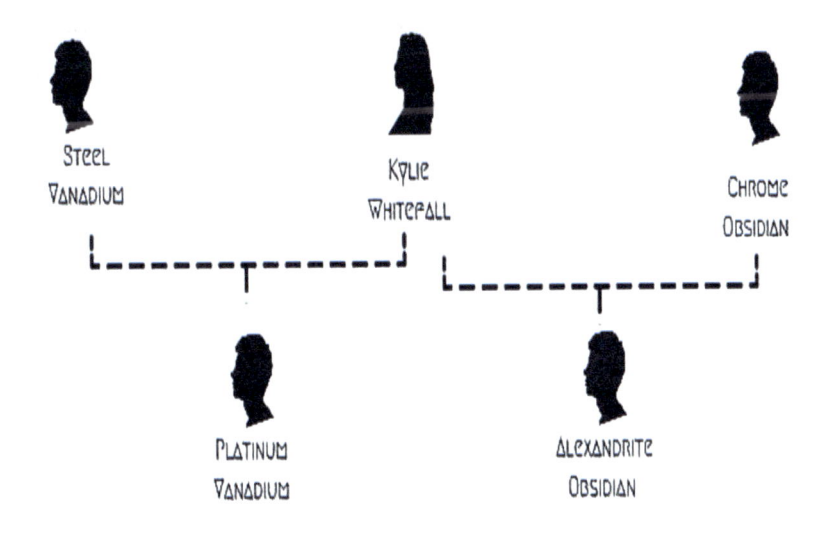

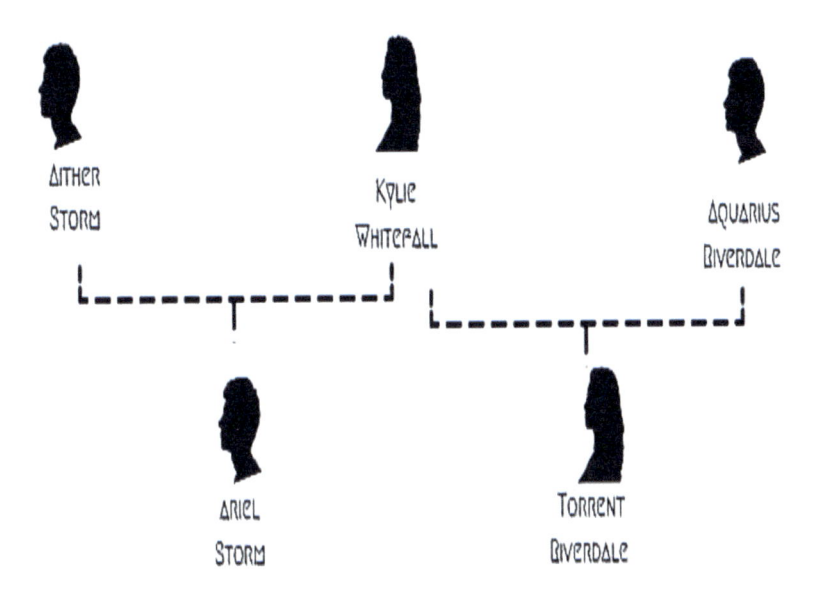

**Steel Vanadium** — **Kylie Whitefall** — **Chrome Obsidian**

- Platinum Vanadium
- Alexandrite Obsidian

**Aither Storm** — **Kylie Whitefall** — **Aquarius Riverdale**

- Ariel Storm
- Torrent Riverdale

# Family Tree

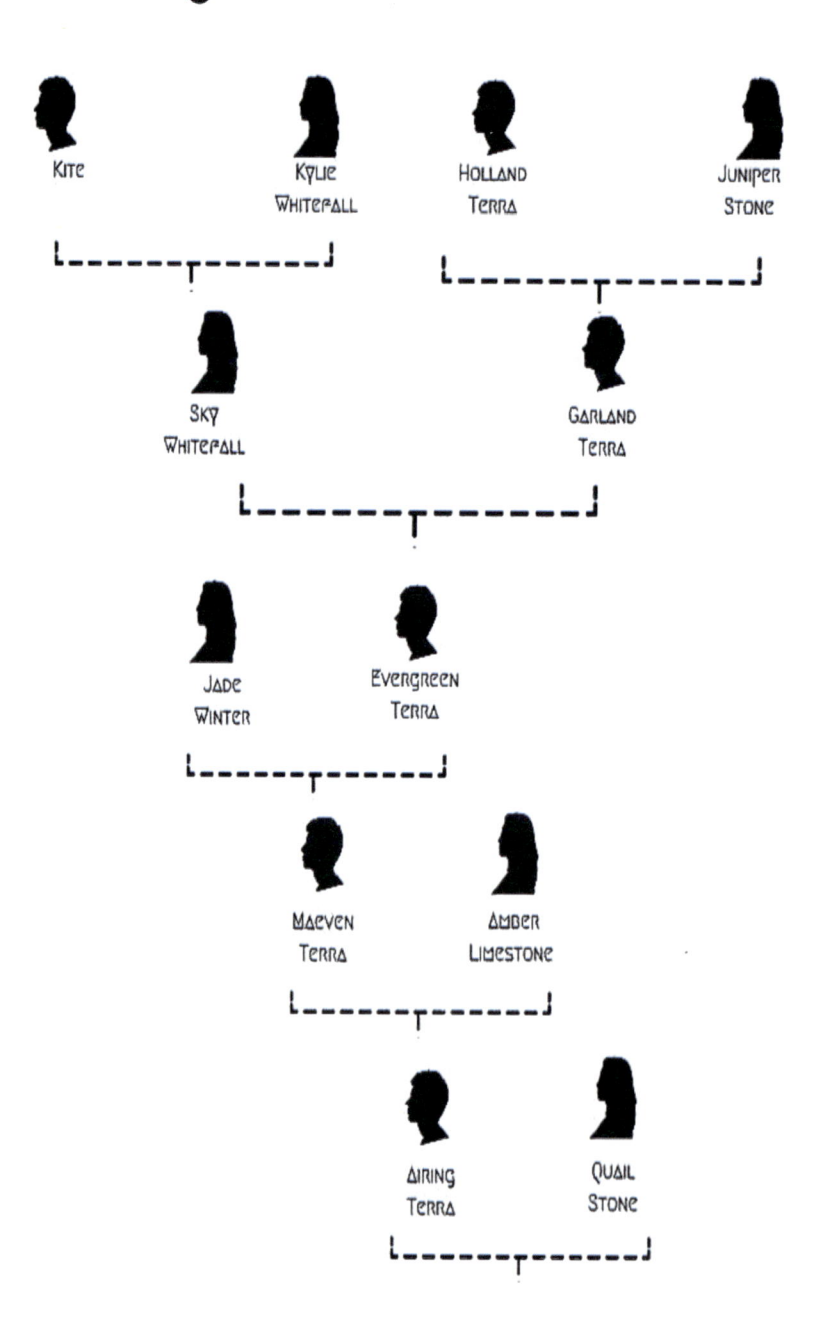

- Kite
- Kylie Whitefall
- Holland Terra
- Juniper Stone

- Sky Whitefall
- Garland Terra

- Jade Winter
- Evergreen Terra

- Maeven Terra
- Amber Limestone

- Airing Terra
- Quail Stone

# Character Profiles
## Kylie

**Birthdate:** Blizzard's Reign, 1685 Imperial Lunar Year

**Faction:** Mage-Born

**Rankings:** Slave, Archduchess

**Stats Chart:**

| | | | | | | | | | |
|---|---|---|---|---|---|---|---|---|---|
| Mage Mana | ■ | ■ | ■ | ■ | ■ | ■ | ■ | ■ | |
| Knight's Aura | | | | | | | | | |
| Adaptability | ■ | ■ | ■ | | | | | | |
| Battle Skill | | | | | | | | | |
| Magic Ability | ■ | ■ | ■ | ■ | ■ | | | | |
| Intellect | ■ | ■ | ■ | ■ | ■ | ■ | ■ | | |

## Character Art

# Realistic Art Character Inspiration

# Character Profiles
## Steel

**Birthdate:** Nivis's End, 1679 Imperial Lunar Year

**Faction:** Knight Faction & Mage-Born

**Rankings:** Duke

**Stats Chart**

|  |  |
|---|---|
| Mage Mana | 9/10 |
| Knight's Aura | 7/10 |
| Adaptability | 10/10 |
| Battle Skill | 7/10 |
| Magic Ability | 10/10 |
| Intellect | 10/10 |

# Character Art

# Realistic Art Character Inspiration

# Character Profiles

## Chrome

**Birthdate:** Moon's Dance, 1679 Imperial Lunar Year

**Faction:** Knight's Faction & Mage-Born

**Rankings:** Archduke

**Stats Chart**

|  |  |
|---|---|
| Mage Mana | ██████████ |
| Knight's Aura | █████████ |
| Adaptability | █████████ |
| Battle Skill | █████████ |
| Magic Ability | ████████ |
| Intellect | ██████████ |

## Character Art

# Realistic Art Character Inspiration

# Character Profiles

## Aquarius

**Birthdate:** Rain's Fall, 1679 Imperial Lunar Year

**Faction:** Knight's Faction & Mage-Born

**Rankings:** Marquess

**Stats Chart**

|  | | | | | | | | | | |
|---|---|---|---|---|---|---|---|---|---|---|
| Mage Mana | ■ | ■ | ■ | ■ | ■ | | | | | |
| Knight's Aura | ■ | ■ | ■ | ■ | | | | | | |
| Adaptability | ■ | ■ | ■ | ■ | ■ | ■ | | | | |
| Battle Skill | ■ | ■ | ■ | ■ | | | | | | |
| Magic Ability | ■ | ■ | ■ | | | | | | | |
| Intellect | ■ | ■ | ■ | ■ | ■ | ■ | ■ | ■ | ■ | ■ |

## Character Art

# Realistic Art Character Inspiration

# Story Timeline

## 1600 Imperial Lunar Year

Drakonians make strides to rebuild, make deals with Arch-Mage in the Mage's Towers, begin blending in with society and humans

## 1679 Imperial Lunar Year

**Nivis's End –** Steel Vanadium is born

**Rain's Fall –** Aquarius Riverdale is born

**Moon's Fall –** Chrome Obsidian is born

## 1682 Imperial Lunar Year

**Spring's Height –** Aither Storm is born

## 1685 Imperial Lunar Year

**Blizzard's Reign –** Ky Stone, AKA Kylie Whitefall is born

## 1696 Imperial Lunar Year

**Year's Fall –** Kite is born

## 1699 Imperial Lunar Year

**Blizzard's Reign –** Chrome saves Ky from slavery, brings her to live at the archduchy

## 1700 Imperial Lunar Year

**Blizzard's Reign –** Chrome, Steel and Aquarius all confess to and begin officially courting Kylie

## 1701 Imperial Lunar Year

**Year's Fall** – Kylie kidnapped by the Wraiths, rescued by Aither, has her powers unsealed, takes Aither as her fourth mate.

## 1702 Imperial Lunar Year

**Blizzard's Reign** – Mating Ceremony with her four mates upon her 18th birthday

**Folias's Blessing** – Safely gives birth to the egg

## 1703 Imperial Lunar Year

**Solaris's Reign** – Egg hatches, Platinum Vanadium is born

## 1706 Imperial Lunar Year

Alexandrite Obsidian is born

## 1709 Imperial Lunar Year

Aerial Storm is born

## 1712 Imperial Lunar Year

Kylie accepts Kite as her 5th and final mate

## 1714 Imperial Lunar Year

Torrent Riverdale is born

## 1716 Imperial Lunar Year

**Veras's Height** – Sky Whitefall is born

## **1730 Imperial Lunar Year**

Sky travels to paternal grandmother's wolf-shifter pack to become alpha pair.

She marries Garland Terra, and they become the alpha pair ruling over the Terra-Stone pack

**MOVING TO THE SHIFTER'S SAGA!**

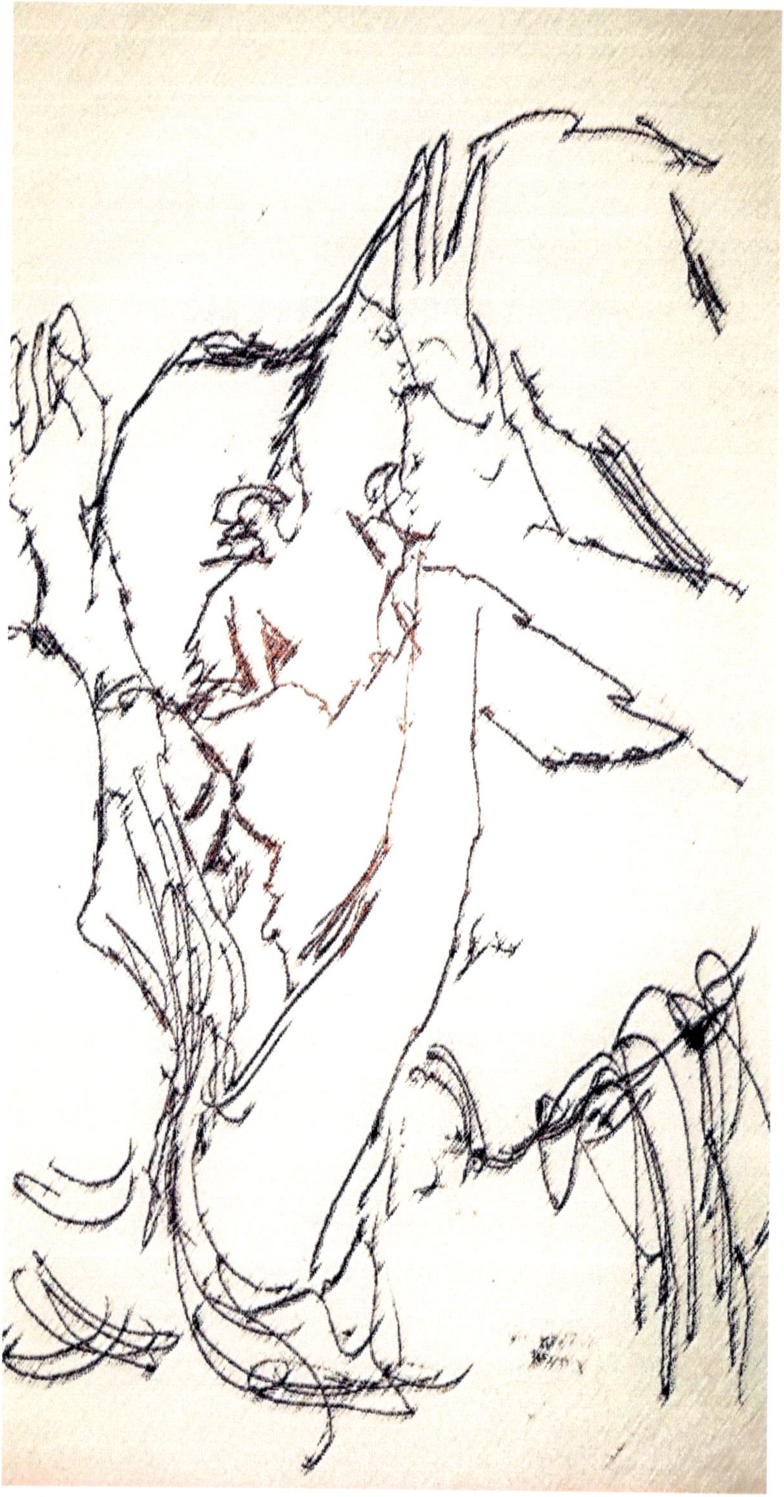

231

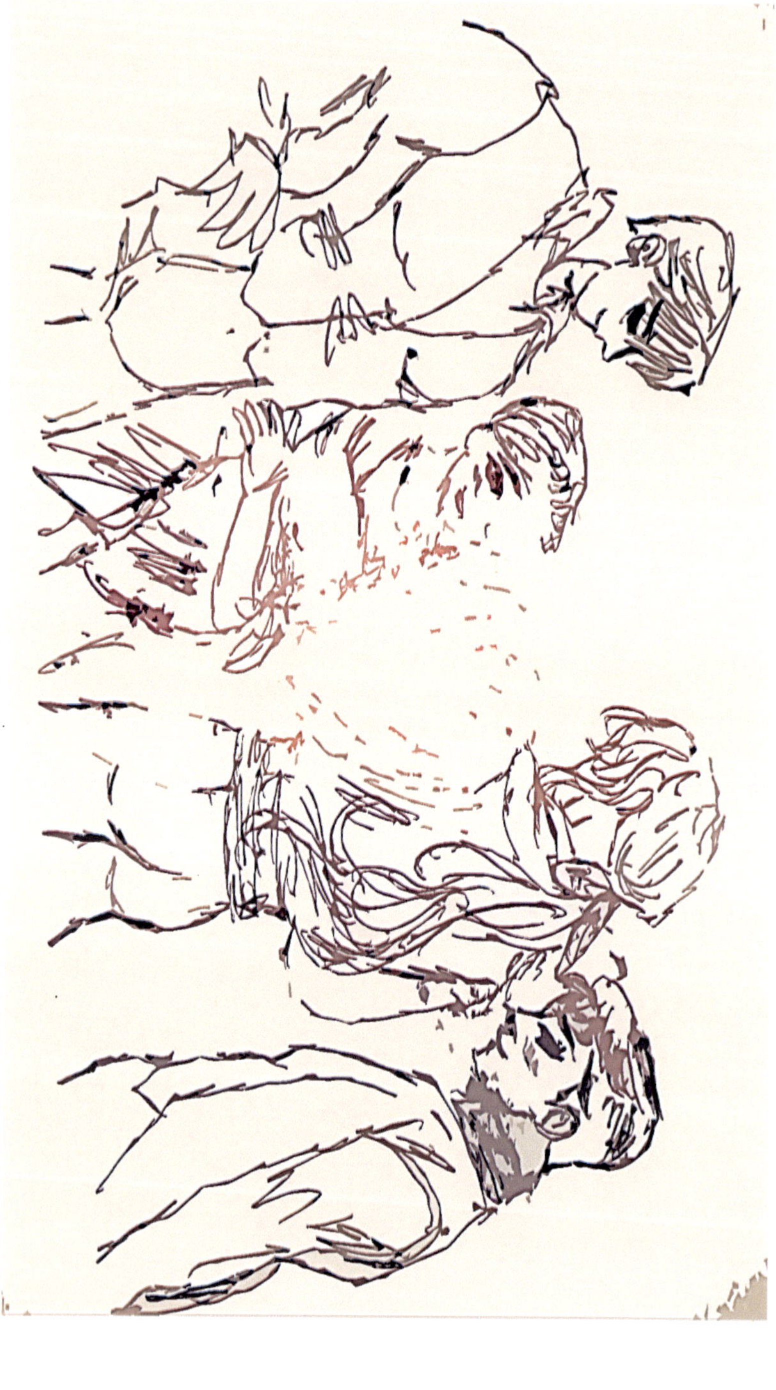

# Story Connections & "Easter Eggs"...

## The Apathetic Knight, Parts 1 & 2

### → The Villainous Princess

Kyeareth + Cinder = Canderoth;

Canderoth created the 5 kingdoms into North, South, East, West and Central, gifting each kingdom to the rule of those close to him.

Northern Kingdom – Cassian Orion, whose descendant, Kerynn Caius (and her uncle) would copulate and create Karmindy.

Western Kingdom – Seryn Leonhart, whose descendant would become Karmindy's step/adopted father.

Southern Kingdom – Kyeareth and Winter, whose descendants would lead to Johannes Valoran.

*The Villainous Princess*

→ *The Disregarded Dragon*

Johannes Valoran IV signs peace and trade agreements with the Mage Faction, bringing in Drakonians. New age begins.

## The Disregarded Dragon

### → The Hidden Queen

Sorcerers from the Drakonian period decided to give power of Truth to two families, with the help of Sorcerers in the Mage Faction.

The "Dark Seer" family and "Light Seer" family now start new era.

## The Hidden Queen
### → The Conquering Empress

Seer Queen tries to kill her husband, so he, as a powerful paladin, changes the power of the Seers with the help of the Mage's Tower in the Mage Faction, and gives Day-Giver and Night-Bringer power to the two ruling families instead of "truth."

Also distributes other abilities to other families to help balance the power out, creating more sorcerers.

Creates the "Seal of Matrimony" for destined partners.

## *The Conquering Empress*

→ *The Abandoned Prince*

Katria fights against abuse from the Night-Bringer kingdom and takes over, creating first Empress-Ruled empire.

Katria + Viorel = Vielle Night-Bringer; Vielle Night-Bringer marries Claudian Jakard, the Crowned Prince of the Jakard Kingdom

*The Abandoned Prince*

→ *The Decoy Duchess*

Claudian Jakard + Vielle Night-Bringer = Claudel Jakard, and Jakard Kingdom's Sultan and Sultana

Klaus, raised by Qassim Malik. Qassim Malik's sister is the mother of Ciel Twilight, in the United Empire, making Klaus and Ciel adopted cousins.

Klaus is cousins with Claudianne Jakard, the daughter of the youngest child of the former sultan, and the new sultan and sultana of the Jakard Kingdom.

Ciel Twilight marries Claudiane's lady-in-waiting, Saffora.

Cavell Jakard is adopted by the Luther Archduke family.

Cavell Jakard Luther's descendants would become the royal family of a small kingdom near the United Empire.

Vander Luther is descended from this family.

Celine Kyle is descended from Kyeareth Severing.

# *The Decoy Duchess*
## → *The Empathetic Brother*

Erich Atkins + Celine Kyle = Erin Atkins.

Erin Atkins + Maria Thompkins = Emilia Atkins

Emilia Atkins marries Marquess James Abraham, and Kathryn Abraham is the illegitimate of "The Empathetic Brother" novel's Marquess Abraham.

Kathryn Abraham marries Killian Jayce, a distant descendant of Asfaloth Ashland (though this is not mentioned in the novel)

## The Empathetic Brother

## → The Anonymous Writer

Asta Fajr, a niece of the Jakard Royal family, is forced to marry Archduke Drake in the United Empire.

Archduke Drake is descended from Marquess Abraham (Kathryn Abraham Soren Jayce's half-brother, who took over the marquessate. This is not mentioned in the novels.)

Asta Fajr + Ashid Zaron = Cadence Drake, AKA "Holy."

Holy marries Constance Markson.

Holy + Constance = Ashar & Asta Markson.

Ashar + Asta Markson = Cadence Markson

Cadence Markson + Emilyn Obsidian = Granite Obsidian

## The Anonymous Writer

## → The Luxurious Slave

Chrome Obsidian is descended from Granite Obsidian

Ky Stone (AKA Kylie Whitefall) is descended from Kysael and Coal's children (Kysael and Coal are from the future prequel saga, The Queen's Saga)

Ky marries Kite (A distant descendant of Kysael and Kynorren, from The Queen's Saga)

Kite + Ky = Sky Whitefall

# The Luxurious Slave

➔ *The Shifter's Saga Book 1.0: The Rejected Lady*

Sky Whitefall moves to her paternal grandmother's wolf shifter pack, the Terra pack, marries a gamma male, and inherits the alpha title.

Sky Whitefall + Garland Terra

We hope you enjoyed The Royal's Saga,
Finale Novella:
**The Royal's Behind the Scenes**
Please join us for the next installment of The Shifter's Saga, Book 1.0–

*The Rejected Lady, Parts 1 & 2...*

Coming soon!
Scheduled for release on
January 15th, 2024!

*Book Excerpt to follow*

KRISTEN ELIZABETH

# The REJECTED Lady

PARTS 1 & 2

*Grandmother and Mother*

*The Shifter's Saga, Book 1.0*

# *Dove...*

"...*Excuse* me?" I asked, glaring at him. "What did you say?"

He scoffed at me. "You know that, don't you? Haven't they taught you anything? Once a male locks in on her scent, his blood and his Moon Mother-given instinct will tell him if she is the right mate for him. He will already be going haywire due to 'the heat;' he won't be thinking about anything but instinct, for the most part. The Moon Mother will give him the knowledge to *know* if she is the right choice as his mate, and if she *is*, he marks her," he said. "Do you know why the mouthy, rude, disrespectful females end up with *weak* males? Because they are *last pick*. Males have already trained their instincts against that female's scent, to smell it as 'bad,' so that she does not attract him when our mating mind wakes up. *No* powerful male wants a she-wolf who *barks* too much, so even if he does become drawn to her scent, those females' true mates reject them and leave them as slim pickings for whatever male might be willing to tolerate her enough to take her," he sneered.

Tears pricked my eyes.

I knew, in that moment, that he was right.

My mother had been worrying herself sick over my mouthy, "lousy attitude" and "strongly voiced opinions."

She knew that I had the *potential* to be desirable, to be first chosen by my true mate because of my bloodline and my pedigree, *but*...

He let me go just as the crunching of snow alerted us to another presence.

"Miss Dove, mister Cloud, the betas have requested your presence," my gamma heir said, out of breath. Then, he noticed our *position*, going pale. "Miss—"

"Let's go, Crow," I told him, sighing. "We will need to talk later."

"I am sorry, Dove, father told me to stay near him because he might send me on an errand. I tried to stay close by in case you needed me, but—"

"How many gamma heirs *does* your pack have?" The boy—Cloud, Crow had called him—asked.

"We only have *one*," I said. "Our pack's only gamma, the Offensive Gamma, has no heirs. So, Alpha Falcon made his second son the Gamma Heir."

"Ah," he said. "My pack only has one gamma, also. *Most* packs have two, but it seems the roles divided evenly between the packs. And since he seems to be your guard, I take it that he is the *Defensive* Gamma Heir, right? Our pack's gamma is the offensive gamma...or, gamma heir only, now. But, once our packs join again, we will have two gammas, as is the norm."

I was basically just ignoring him, at this point. He was already thinking that he was going to take my position, and thinking badly of me as a potential mate.

I didn't want to talk to him.

We walked to the front of the pack house, and into the great-room, where our alphas and betas were waiting for us.

"Ah, good," his alpha said. "You have arrived. Thank you, young Defensive Gamma Heir," he said to Crow, who gave a nod and went to sit by his side.

"We have something important to discuss with you both," my uncle said. "As your fathers may have told you, the other packs in the state have been fighting over territory lately, and it seems that several of the packs have set their eyes on our territory," he said, looking grave. "So, in response, we have decided to reunite with our brother pack. However, there is a bit of a…stipulation to rejoining packs. No pack has ever had two alphas or two betas. Two gammas are standard, but no rank above that. Also, to rejoin, we have to…rejoin the bloodline entirely."

The other alpha spoke up again. "Because the original alpha of the joined packs had twin sons who then split the packs and married their own mates, it split the bloodline into two as well. To rejoin, our shaman has asked for a sign to learn how this will be possible in a peaceful way and not struggle with the ranking system. The first condition is something that we had never taken into consideration without it being the Moon Mother's choice, but…"

"There has to be a *marriage*," a male I didn't recognize said.

"A *marriage*, father?" Cloud asked, and I saw the resemblance as he said it.

*So, this was their pack's beta male.*

"Yes," he said. "Normally, we wait for a wolf to turn fourteen—age two, for your *wolf*—and let their senses given by the Moon Mother choose their true mates. As I am sure you both know, when you turn seven years of age, you awaken and meet your wolf, whom has just turned one-year-old, in your own body. Whatever female or male you may find as a mate will also start to seem more desirable and you will sense their presence around you or their scent might be particularly nice. When you turn fourteen and your wolf is two, the 'mating mind' awakens, and the instinct to mate with your fated partner drives you to find and accomplish this mating, immediately. An arranged marriage is highly unorthodox and considered rude to the Moon Mother…however, the only way to rejoin the blood and the pack together peacefully is through marriage."

It is rare for a true mate to be found outside of one's own pack, so an arrangement *was* necessary for this to happen...but...

"So, what does that have to do with *us*?" Cloud beat me to asking, deadpanning.

"*Well*," my father wouldn't look at me, and I understood even before the words escaped his mouth. "Both packs, we..." He sighed. "The Terra-Stone pack has a male alpha heir who is, unfortunately, weak and sick and isn't fit to command...so he has refused. But we *do* have a male beta heir, and male offensive gamma heir. *None* of those families have a *female*. The Terra-Forest pack has a male alpha heir, a male gamma heir, but *not*...*a female beta child*."

Cloud gaped, whirling his eyes to me. "You...you mean to marry *me* to *her*?" He asked, stunned.

His father nodded, looking at us sheepishly. "*She* is the *only* female close to your age who is of similar rank in *their* pack, son. We were also worried that she would feel intimidated by you joining their pack and taking her position from her—"

"I would *never* choose her!" Cloud said, a slight growl to his undertones. "She wouldn't be the Moon Mother's choice for me, either, I am sure of it. She might be *pretty*, but *no* self-respecting, powerful beta male would fall for a girl with *that* mouth or *attitude*—"

"We will spend the next two years working with her, *seriously*, fixing her behavior and attitude. She is ten now, but will be eleven in April. In two years, she will be turning thirteen. It just only a year shy of when your wolves would choose mates anyway, so it won't be a drastic change to the norm. You will be given medication to keep you from smelling your mate, so even though you will come of age before she will, it will not become an issue for you to be concerned with, and we can proceed as planned—"

"But I—" Cloud tried, but his father glared at him.

"Father, you can't do this—" I tried.

"Stop it, Dove!" He scolded.

"But—"

"We *have* to reunite the packs," his alpha interrupted. "This is how we do it *peacefully*. You two are the key to that! A very important role! You should feel honored!" He said. Cloud and I glared at one another, and the alpha continued. "At the ceremony, the most powerful of the alphas will take command of the united pack, the most powerful beta will become the new alpha's beta, and *you* will be groomed to become the beta of the combined packs with your new beta female. As your alpha and as your uncle, I'm sure you know that I do not wish to have to use my alpha blood to *force* you into submission, but if I have to—"

"*No*," Cloud said, kneeling and baring his neck in submission to his alpha. "That is unnecessary. I will do as I am told. It is in my blood, as a trueborn beta heir, to obey the alpha's decisions."

Our alphas both nodded, before alpha Falcon turned his attention to me. "Is this going to be a problem, Dove?"

I glanced at Cloud, who looked up at me from the corner of his eye. A sour look crossed his face when I didn't answer right away.

"**Dove**!" Falcon said, and I could feel the pressure of force in his tone. What—?

He had never used his alpha pressure on me before, so I had no idea what it felt like and how to respond.

As it turns out, I had no ability to respond in any graceful manner, it seemed.

I gasped, collapsing to my knees...and I was shocked completely when Cloud quickly reached to catch me before my face hit the floor.

He helped me straighten a bit, waiting for me.

Why wasn't the pressure lessening...?

"...Bare your neck and submit," Cloud murmured into my ear. "You have to submit to the alpha."

I glanced at him, and he gave me a nod, helping me sit up a little more...and I bared my neck in submission to the alpha.

"...No, alpha. No problems."

As soon as I submitted, the pressure lifted.

I was successfully trapped.

I felt tears sting my eyes, even as I felt Cloud helping me to stand as we were dismissed, while my mind was stuck in a haze...and the cold wind blasted my face as he walked me outside. I gasped, struggling to breathe.

"That was your first time under the alpha command, I take it," Cloud said, soft. "It gets easier to take it, but the first few times—especially before your wolf fully awakens as an adult—is extremely difficult. You did fairly well, considering."

I didn't want to be comforted by him.

I wanted to shift, to run far away, but shifting was very personal.

Only your mate was supposed to see you strip and shift.

I was sure that this boy who disliked me would see me shift soon enough, anyway, since he was now my fiancé, but for now...I wanted to keep my wolf to myself.

A *mother* was there for her daughter's first shift, and a father was there for his son's first shift, but outside of that, the shift, itself, was private.

We did do pack runs often, admiring our beautiful wolves together, but shifting was painful and powerful and a wolf's basest instinct was to be alone during that change, unless their mate was there.

Wolves were at their most vulnerable during their shift, and it was one of the best times to kill one of us.

If you weren't *completely trusting* of whomever you were with, you didn't want to shift with anyone around.

I didn't think I would ever *want* to shift in front of Cloud, especially not right now.

"Are you alright, Dove?" Crow asked, flitting about me in a worried manner.

"Get her home," I heard Cloud tell him. "I imagine she's probably overwhelmed. I know *I* am not entirely pleased, but—"

"I won't get a Moon Mother given true mate," I whispered, voice trembling and eyes watery. "Even if I have one...I can't even be with him."

Cloud scoffed. "*That's* what upsets you? It isn't like *you're* the only one struggling. You're such a selfish child! How do you think I feel? *I'm* the one who has to be with a female I wouldn't have chosen! You are getting the better end of the deal, here! I am a powerful, desirable, attractive male! I am extremely popular and helpful to my pack. I would take care of you and honor you! You're so selfish! This is about much more than your petty *feelings*. It isn't like *I'm* thrilled, either."

I seethed, blushing hard as bristled and I glared at him. "I know you aren't happy about this, but *I* was raised being taught that I would be chosen by a powerful male if I worked hard to become his heart's desire, and that the Moon Mother would reward me for loving my pack with a male that was beautiful and powerful and would *love* me more than anything. That he would...see *me* as a Moon Mother, because I was given to him by the Moon Mother..." Tears started to spill down my cheeks, and I turned away. "That he would love me as much as my father loves my mother. That it would be an all-encompassing, and that nobody else would ever be able to offer me that level of love. I just...wanted what he promised..."

He didn't respond to that.

"But as you have clearly stated, you would *never* pick me, and you seem sure the Moon Mother wouldn't pick me for you, either."

I whipped around to face him, and he gaped at me and my tear-streaked face.

"Dove—"

"That can only mean that *I* won't be *special* to you." I looked at him to see him look...almost conflicted. "It means that you won't even be *able* to love me the way that...well, even if I attracted a *weaker* mate, I am sure he would have at least *loved* me, wouldn't he?"

"Dove-"

"But *you*...you won't be able to give me love. You might act dutifully and you might take care of me and give me pups, but beyond that, you will spend your life resenting me...and I'll spend my life heartbroken with a male who can't even want me, let alone love me as the Moon Mother intended for me to be loved...I have to give up being loved, just to be of use to the pack. No other wolves will understand having to compromise that. Only us. And that's heartbreaking." I turned away again. "It was nice to meet you, beta heir Cloud. I will do my best to be less of a disappointment to you the next time we meet."

Then, I ran away, and I didn't let myself stop until I reached my bed.

..................
......................
............................

............................Want to keep reading?

Be sure keep an eye out for the release of
**The Shifter's Saga, Book 1.0:**
**The Rejected Lady, Parts 1 & 2!**

It only gets better from here, and let us not forget: STEAMIER.

...Y

U...

...M

# Books by Kristen Elizabeth

## >The Royal's Saga<

The Apathetic Knight, Part 1 – The Crowning
The Apathetic Knight, Part 2 – The Burning
The Apathetic Knight, Part 3 – The Freezing
The Villainous Princess, Part 1 – The Trapped
The Villainous Princess, Part 2 – The Freed
The Disregarded Dragon
The Hidden Queen
The Conquering Empress
The Abandoned Prince
The Decoy Duchess
The Empathetic Brother
The Anonymous Writer
The Luxurious Slave
The Incensed Guardian Novella
**>The Royal's Behind the Scenes Finale Novella<**

## The Shifter's Saga

The Rejected Lady Book 1: Parts 1 & 2
The Rejected Lady Book 2: Parts 3 & 4

…Further titles coming soon!

## The Lover's Saga

Titles coming soon!

## The Spell-Caster's Saga

Titles coming soon!

## The Dreamer's Saga

Titles coming soon!

## The Queen's Saga

Titles coming soon!

## The Knight's Saga

Titles coming soon!

## The Immortal's Saga

Titles coming soon!

## The Villain's Saga

Titles coming soon!

## The Children's Saga (PG13)

Titles coming soon!

# Acknowledgments

A special thanks to my proof reader & good friend, Trisha, for reading through the novels and helping me with the grammatical and spelling aspects. Without your help, there were a lot of mistakes that would have made it into the books, and you encouraged me a ton. Thank you for your interest and investment in the story! I love you.

A thanks to the Ghost-Writer who helped me with some editing, some of the ideas, and some of the bonus content added to the original story. You rock, and I appreciate that. Thank you so much!

A special thanks to those who supported my work, including but not limited to, Sammie-Anne, Shannon, Amber, and so on. Several people who really encouraged me to write, publish and seek higher things. You guys inspired me to make this possible. I appreciate it so much. Special thanks goes to my most avid of fans, including Christine, Jeanna, and a few others who had been following my work and have gone to extra measures above and beyond to support and read my works.

All of you aforementioned people make writing the books so much more exciting so that I can see your reactions and give you good books to read!

Thank you all for being amazing. Without you, there is no way I would have gotten such a great start!

A special thanks to my husband, Reece, for allowing me to take so much time to write and keeping everything running, and not complaining a ton.

You wanted me to pursue my goals, and I needed that extra push because I'm bad about procrastinating on things. I love you, handsome ;)

I want to give a special thanks to my mom. You don't read my work or really think this will go that far, but you love me and try to support me the best you can. Thank you for everything, and I love you.

I, lastly, want to thank those of my followers who have stuck by me through multiple re-writes, re-publishing, and who have been patient with me and stuck it out to support me. I know that it has been a long journey that started on December 21$^{st}$, 2022.

Thank you for your support for the last year, and I hope you will continue to follow my work! Now that I know what I'm doing and have finished going through the growing pains, learning difficulties and struggles.

You all are awesome, and I love you all.

Thank you all so much <3

# About the Author

Kristen Elizabeth is now on social media! Follow on Instagram and Tiktok! Handle for both apps is

## lovelymadness92

She also has an author's page on Facebook! Check her out at

## Kristen Elizabeth
## (Lovely Madness Fantasies)

Follow for more bonus content, updates, and publishing schedules!

Kristen spent the majority of her life emersed in arts and music, and used writing and reading as an opportunity to escape from the trauma and depression that spiraled out of control from the background that she crawled out of.

Writing, arts and music opened up an entirely new world for her, and she kept herself surrounded by it to avoid the stress and anxiety that was forcing down on her.

Kristen, herself, is also on the Autism Spectrum, and wants to share her unique worlds with those around her.

She hopes someone out there will enjoy her creations as much as she does and use her creations to escape from the mundane everyday life.

Kristen's biggest goal is to fit somewhere outside of the norm, and to broaden horizons in the world of fiction.

Life isn't always happy endings, sunshine, and rainbows.

Sometimes, life is an utter freakshow and things don't work out the way you hoped.

That's something that Kristen wants to bring to her writing.

**Let Kristen help you fall into her world of Lovely Madness ;)**

None of this happens without the readers! Please help me by sharing and spreading the word means so much to me!

Thank you so much!

I hope you tune in for The Shifter's Saga, Book 1.0:
**The Rejected Lady, Parts 1 & 2!**

# Please join me as we delve into the next series:

# The Shifter's Saga!

Are you tired of the same-old-same-old stories you find in today's werewolf novels?

I know that I am!

As it happens, I love shifter stories, but most of them, I find myself desperate for a new plot line or a different trope.

That is my goal with this coming series!

It won't be like anything else you have read, because sometimes…

Sometimes, love has to be found in the wildest and maddest of places.

Join me for an all new kind of *lovely madness.*

Coming soon!

# Kristen Elizabeth

## The Royal's Saga

In honor of Relaunching
The Royal's Saga,
I will be Rapid-Realeasing the novels
throughout the remainder of the
year 2023, in anticipation of the
release of
The Shifter's Saga
Coming January, 2024!
Follow me for more!
@ lovelymadness92
Insta & tiktok!

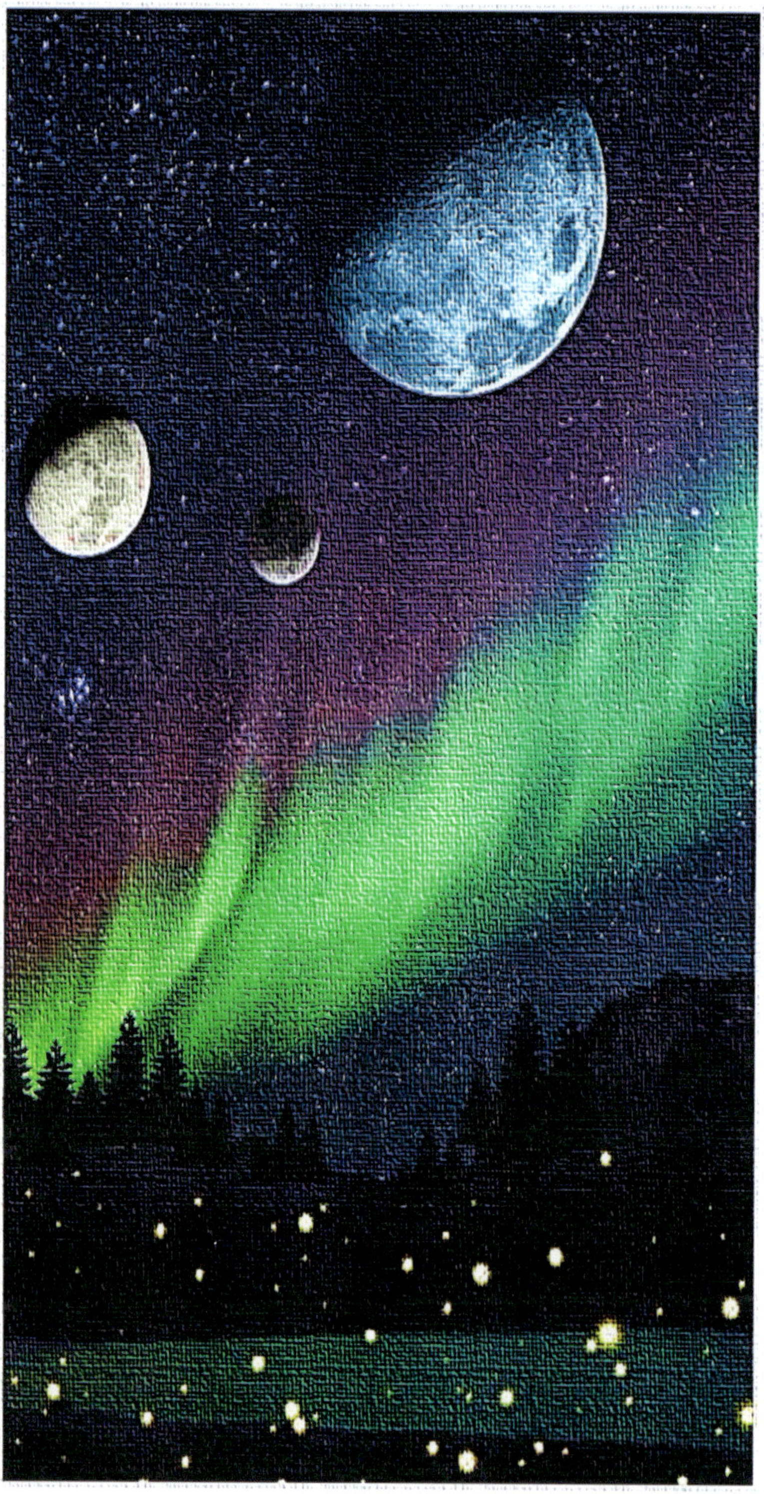

# Kristen Elizabeth
## Letting you fall into a world of Lovely Madness

# What to look forward to in the next saga:

## Werewolves
Wolf-shifters and Lycans!

## Wraiths
Vampires!

## Other shifters
Cat-shifters, Big Cat shifters, dog shifters and more!

## Other Supernatural Creatures
Mermaids

# Lovely Madness Fantasies

**Kristen Elizabeth**
FANTASY ROMANCE AUTHOR

# Final Remarks

Thank you so much for reading Kristen Elizabeth's novel world of Lovely Madness

The Royal's Saga,

Finale Novella:

The Royal's Behind the Scenes

1st Edition;

"Author's Art Edition."

See you in the next saga!

*Kristen Elizabeth*

Made in the USA
Columbia, SC
26 May 2024